The Boy Who Grew Antlers

Becky Clark

ISBN 979-8-9896967-0-3 (PB)
ISBN 979-8-9896967-1-0 (E-Book)

First Printing, 2024

The Boy Who Grew Antlers

For Mark.
Thank you for all your incredible and wonderful support.
You're my favorite.

And for Little MAC III.
You can stop kicking Momma's belly any time now.

One

The Boy Who Grew Antlers

1

The Boy Who Took His Mom to Career Day

Andy

I am so nervous. Everyone came to class today.

The other fifth grade class came to our classroom too.

And teachers from other classes.

And the vice principal.

And the principal.

Mom is sitting at the front of the room, in one of the student desk chairs, which is a little smaller than the adult chairs, and I am standing next to her. It feels weird to be standing there. For a lot of reasons. For starters, I'm a little taller than Mom when she's sitting in a too-short chair. I don't like being taller than her. Then, everyone from both fifth grade classes is sitting on the floor, so now I'm taller than them too. The desks were pushed against the walls to make more room for everyone, and they brought extra rugs to put on the floor, so everyone isn't sitting on the dirty floor tiles. Teachers are standing around the edges and in the back of the room. I can see them whispering to each other and smiling. They all look excited but also nervous. I've seen other adults act like that before when they meet Mom.

Mom takes my shoulder and gives it a gentle squeeze. I turn to her and see she's smiling at me. She leans in just a little and whispers, "You got this, bud."

I'm scared for a second she's going to give me a kiss on the cheek, but she doesn't. She kept her promise not to kiss me in front of my classmates and teachers. I turn back around to face the class...the *classes*.

"Um, hello, everyone," I say to the room. Everyone's still talking and whispering. No one heard me.

Mom squeezes my shoulder again. "A little louder, bud. You can do it."

"Hello, everyone!" I say, much louder. Maybe too loud. Everyone suddenly goes quiet and turns to face us. I continue my introduction. "My name is Andy Bennett, and I would like to introduce my mom, Abby Andrews. She is a professional movie actress and Muse, and she is here to talk about her career and what it was like to be a Muse in movies." I look at Mom again, in case there is something I forgot to say.

"That was perfect, bud," she says to me with her big smile.

I nod and sit on the floor next to her, still facing the class. This is so much better. Now I'm not so tall.

"Well, first, let me thank all of you for inviting me to your Career Day," Mom begins. She doesn't stand up in front of the class like the other parents have done at the other Career Day presentations. She told Mrs. Perkins she was okay with sitting the whole time. I thought that was kinda weird, and maybe I should have told her that the other parents all stood up for their presentations. "Your teacher, Mrs. Perkins, had a great idea that I should start by explaining to all of you what exactly a Muse is and does," she continues, "so I hope you don't mind if we start with a little history lesson."

The adults laugh kinda quietly. Only a few of my classmates laugh. I just smile and sit with my legs crossed next to Mom's chair. I've heard this story before. I don't mind it. It's kinda interesting.

"So, a Muse is someone who can change parts of their body and make them look different," Mom explains. "You'll hear people say we alter or transform our aesthetic, which is just a fancy way of saying we can change the shapes of parts of our bodies. The earliest record of Muses was found in Japanese writings and paintings. Experts say these records are over 800 years old. You can see some of these paintings in museums. There are depictions of models or actors with obviously exaggerated features, like long fingers, bigger ears, things like that. A couple hundred years after that, paintings from different European countries had people or subjects with similar exaggerated features, like bigger cheeks, longer chins, pointed ears, and the like.

"Then, in the late 1700s, doctors started to write books about what they called the 'Muse Phenomenon.'" Mom uses her fingers to make quote marks in the air when she says "Muse Phenomenon." She got that from Gramma. "A lot of people back then thought people who could change their bodies were possessed by demons, but doctors who researched and worked with people who could do this found out it was perfectly safe and natural, and not dangerous to anyone's body if they did it right. Obviously, if you do something wrong, it can hurt a lot, but that's why I do what I do now, which is to teach actors how to work with Creators to be a Muse safely."

Riley, one of the girls from my class, raises her hand and asks quietly, "What's a Creator?"

"Ah, a Creator is kinda like an artist who sculpts," Mom answers. "Only they don't sculpt clay but, rather, they work with Muses to, in a way, sculpt our bodies. Basically, a Creator has the vision for the Muse, and the Muse makes themselves into that vision. When a Muse works with a Creator that they get along with really, really well, that Muse can not only perform amazing transformations, they're much safer on the Muse too. The Creator I worked with for a long, long time—his name is Walter Saint James—has been a mentor and one of my best friends for many, many years. What he does is, he looks at a character that I'm going to play in a movie, and then he looks at me. He first looks at things like where my shoulders are, where my feet are, where my knees and elbows are, and basically how I fit together. We then work together on where I can make things grow or change shape so that I can look more like the character. For example, I did a movie once where I was part fish, so I needed to have gills on my neck. I can't just grow them anywhere—it might not look right. So my friend Walter helped me find where exactly on my neck they had to be, how long they had to be, what the texture of them should be, and things like that."

"What else have you grown?" Jason, one of the boys from the other class, blurts out.

Several kids laugh and I can see a couple teachers get uncomfortable. Mom laughs a little at the question too. The teachers don't know that Mom doesn't get mad very easily. I've asked way weirder questions before.

"Well," Mom answers, "one of my first transformations was growing pointy elf ears. You kids may be too young to remember a movie called *Catastrophe on Christmas Eve.*" Several teachers and a lot of my classmates smile and clap. I'm not really that surprised that a lot of them recognize the movie, since it still plays on TV every year around Christmas. We watched it in one of my classes one year on the last day of school before Christmas break, when our teacher didn't want to teach anything that day. Of course, no one in that class knew that it was my mom in the movie. We don't have the same last name. My teacher knew, though. He told the class afterward, and everyone looked at me weird the rest of the day.

"Who were you in that movie?" Mike yells out from the back of the classroom.

"She was Sadie, the clumsy elf, dummy!" Tracy, who is sitting up in the front, yells out over her shoulder. Tracy was in my class when we watched the movie. "She's the one who dropped all the presents out of Santa's sleigh, remember?"

"Oh wow!" Mike exclaims. "You were in a movie with Santa?"

Everyone in the class laughs. The adults laugh more than my classmates at Mike's comment.

"No," Mom replies very nicely. "That was just an actor playing Santa that time. I haven't gotten to be in a movie with Santa yet."

"So, can you, like, grow more arms or, like, grow another head or something?" Paul asks.

"Not exactly," Mom says. "A human body has a lot of parts that make it up, like skin, organs, bones, muscles, tendons, and all that, right? You know how your ears and nose don't have bones or muscles in them? Your ears and nose are made of what's called cartilage, and that's basically what's growing out of the body. We call those growths 'transformations.' Transformations can be hard or soft, thick or thin, long or short, almost anything we want. And with a lot of practice, a Muse can make some really crazy transformations. Like, once I created transformations that looked like extra arms for an alien I had to play. They put me in a jacket with extra arm holes, which helped make it look like they were real arms, but I couldn't move them on my own. They just kinda stuck out straight like this." Mom demonstrates what her fake arms looked like by holding her real arms straight out of her side. She makes sure not to hit me in the head when she does that, even though my head is about at her arm height. Mom then leans back and forth like she's a stiff robot keeping her arms straight out. My classmates laugh. I kinda laugh too.

"What was the hardest thing you had to grow for a movie?" Sal asks.

Mom pauses for a second to think, but I already know what she's going to say. "Probably the time I grew wings. That was really, really hard, because they were super big, and I had to grow feathers too."

A lot of my classmates gasp. A lot of the adults are nodding. Most of the adults who come to talk to Mom always want to talk to her about the wings movie. Mom wouldn't let me see the movie until I turned nine. She and Dad thought it would be too scary for me. I wasn't scared when I saw it, but the part in the movie where Mom had to grow wings looked, well, super creepy. Dad doesn't like to watch that part of the movie. Actually, now that I think about it, Dad doesn't like to watch that movie at all.

"What happens when you want to get rid of the stuff you grow?" Maddy asks. "Do you have to cut it off or something?"

"If you do it right, you can just leave it, and it will go away on its own," Mom answers. "For me, it's when I go to sleep. But sometimes people have had to get doctors to help. Mostly those people didn't know what they were doing, which is why, again, I work to teach people how to transform safely. People don't want to have parts of them surgically removed if they don't have to, you know?"

"Can you teach me to grow stuff on my face?" Mike blurts out again. The whole class laughs again.

Mom answers while also laughing, "Actually, I might." The class gasps, and a lot of the kids start to smile excitedly. "But," Mom quickly says, "not yet. You're all way too young, and kids definitely shouldn't be creating transformations on themselves. It's way too dangerous. But that's really the limit, right? Becoming a Muse is a skill like any other. Some people are born with the ability to do it easily, while others, they need to study and practice a lot more before they get it. Like painting or learning an instrument. Back in the day, doctors wondered if the talent was genetic—meaning you were born with it or inherited it from your parents—but with recent studies, they've determined that there's no real reason why anyone couldn't do it. However, as I said before, it's extremely dangerous if you don't know what you're doing. Andy, I'm sure, could tell you, I always show him examples of when people try to transform some part of their body and it goes very, very wrong—so wrong they have to have surgery or it permanently disfigures them somehow—because he knows I don't want him to do anything so dangerous."

Mom's right. Any time she sees a story in the news or a magazine, she shows it to me, and I have to promise her I'll never do what that other person did. Sometimes she's very angry (but not at me) and sometimes she's very, very sad. One time, she was telling me about a young girl who tried to change her face because she thought she wasn't pretty enough, and she ended up having to have her nose removed because her transformation was pulling on her face too much, and she couldn't undo it. Mom was angry crying when she showed me that story. Then she hugged me for a long time. So, yeah, Mom's very, very serious that she doesn't want to see me try any transformations before I'm grown up.

"So," Mom says, "if you're still super interested in trying a transformation, you probably can. But, not for another seven or eight years, and definitely not without the help of someone who can show you how to do it safely. That includes creating the transformation *and* safely removing it. You need to know how to do both to be safe and not hurt yourself."

Everyone's quiet for a few seconds. I see teachers nodding, and some of the kids, who looked excited before, now look a little scared.

Then, Tracy asks, "What's it like to be famous?"

"Um..." Mom starts. She does have an answer for this, too, but she's still thinking about it before she talks. I heard Mom tell Dad at dinner last night that she figured someone would ask this question on Career Day. She doesn't like when people ask her this in interviews, but she told Dad she would still try and answer the question if one of my classmates asked. "First, being famous and being an actress and Muse are different things. I like being an actress, and I had fun being a Muse, for sure. I got to get dressed up and act in fun movies and meet a lot of really neat and creative people. Being famous, though, means I'm recognized by people I don't know, and I have to be in front of people sometimes when I don't want to be, and talk to people I don't want to talk to. Being famous is actually not a lot of fun. Sometimes I would rather be sitting at home watching TV or making dinner for my family."

"My dad says you're ugly."

The class goes silent when Bruno says this out loud. I can see teachers trying to shoosh him from the edges, and a lot of my classmates start whispering to each other. I can feel myself getting angry and my cheeks turning hot. I want to punch him in the face. Who says stuff like that in front of everyone? I look up at Mom, ready to see her mad too.

She's the only one in the room smiling and laughing.

"Well, Bruno," Mom says, "you tell your dad that I think you are ten times more handsome than he is."

Everyone in the room, even the teachers, burst out laughing. Even I start laughing. Bruno turns bright red and lowers his head into his chest.

My classmates probably don't know Mom used to work with Bruno's dad when they were younger. Bruno's dad used to be an actor, but he wasn't a Muse like Mom. My dad calls Bruno's dad a Hollywood "pretty boy," but sometimes he will accidentally say "petty boy" instead. It makes Mom laugh whenever he does.

Mrs. Perkins makes her way to the front of the room and calms the class down. Everyone's still laughing. Even me. "Okay, everyone. Settle down. Settle. Paul, stop pointing. You, too, Riley. Alright, Andy's mom has to leave pretty soon, but do we have any more questions for Miss Andrews before she has to go?"

"Can you transform something for us?" Mike calls out. He doesn't even raise his hand.

Others in the class clap and cheer, saying things like, "Yeah, let's see! Let's see!" It doesn't look like the teachers are trying to stop them. I think they want to see Mom transform too.

Mom puts her hands up and quiets everyone down, even the teachers. She closes her eyes and starts leaning her head a bit to the side. I've seen her do this before. It's actually really neat. After a few seconds, while everyone is watching her very quietly, she opens her eyes, smiles, and moves her hair around her ear. She has shaped her right ear into Sadie the Elf's unique shape—pointed, with the tip curled forward a little. Everyone is super impressed and starts clapping and cheering. Everyone except Bruno, who still has his head down.

Mom puts her hair down, hiding her ear again, and stands up to thank Mrs. Perkins. I get up, too, and stand next to them. Mom puts her hand on my shoulder and again gives it a gentle squeeze.

"Let's thank Miss Andrews again for taking time out of her busy schedule to come to our class and talk to all of us," Mrs. Perkins says to the room. Everyone claps again. "And let's thank Andy for introducing his mother to everyone." Not as many people clap for me. Mostly the teachers and some of my classmates. Bruno looks more angry at me.

Then, the principal, Mr. Foldger, who was standing in the very back of the room, raises his hand and asks if Mom would take a picture with all the kids in the class. Mom agrees very happily. She holds onto both my shoulders this time, as if to make sure I don't get lost in the crowd, as everyone rushes to the front of the room to stand as close as they can to her. Somehow, Mr. Foldger manages to wrangle every kid into place to take a few pictures on his phone. Everyone claps for Mom one more time before Mr. Foldger and I walk with her out of the classroom.

Mom holds my hand as we walk down the hall to the front entrance. Mr. Foldger thanks Mom at least twenty times while we're walking. He asks her if she would come visit again and share more stories, possibly for all the students and faculty in the school. Mom politely says she'll "consider his request," and then asks if she can borrow me as her escort to the main entrance and wait with her until her ride comes. Mr. Foldger agrees, as long as I "promptly returned to class afterward."

Mom and I walk out the front doors of the school and sit on the top step outside the entrance where we can watch the parking lot for her ride. She's flying to Canada in a few hours to go work with the actors on a TV show that's being filmed out there. She's going to be gone for a week. I'm going to miss her. I always miss her when she's away for a long time. But I don't tell her that because I'm too embarrassed.

"So, how'd I do?" she asks. I get the feeling she's actually worried she did a bad job.

"I think that was good," I say, trying to be reassuring. "I wish there weren't so many people in the classroom, though. I don't like talking in front of a lot of people."

"I know, sweetheart," she replies, rubbing my back. "You were perfect up there. I just want to make sure I don't embarrass you. I know I'm kind of a weird Mom to have, and people can act differently when I'm around."

"I didn't feel embarrassed," I say, and I mean it. "I just get nervous talking in front of lots of people. But you're great at it."

Mom smiles. She looks relieved.

Mom's ride rounds the corner and turns into the school parking lot. Mom and I stand up and walk down the steps to the curb where the car is pulling up. She kneels down next to me to say goodbye. She's shorter than me again, and it still feels weird. "Now, you take care of your dad while I'm away," she says as she always does before leaving for a long trip. "Don't let him get into trouble, and don't give him any trouble. You boys are my world, okay?"

"Okay..." That statement never made sense to me. What does she mean I was her "world"?

Miss Reynolds, Mom's assistant, gets out of the passenger seat of the car to open the back door for Mom. Mom never likes being driven to places, or having doors opened for her, but she never lets her assistants know. Miss Reynolds is new, too, and probably doesn't know when to open doors for Mom and when Mom wants to open her own door. Mom will tell me when she's working with someone new that she wishes I was there to tell them what she likes and what she doesn't like, since I somehow always know. It's the same around Christmas and her birthday, too, when Dad's trying to find the right gift for her.

"You be good," she says, then kisses my cheek. "Take care of your father," she says, then kisses my other cheek. "Don't get into trouble," she says, then kisses my first cheek again. "I love you very, very much," she says, then kisses my forehead.

"I love you too," I say softly, hoping nobody can hear me say that but Mom.

Mom stands up straight again and walks to the car. She thanks Miss Reynolds for opening the door for her and gets into the back seat. Miss Reynolds looks happy and relieved when Mom thanks her. I wave to Mom one more time before the door closes, then wave to Miss Reynolds. Miss Reynolds gives me a nice smile and waves back before getting back into the passenger seat and closing her door. I like Miss Reynolds. She's one of Mom's nicer assistants.

I make sure the car pulls completely out of the parking lot and is far down the street before I wipe all Mom's kisses off my face and head back to my classroom. I love Mom very much, but she kisses me way too much.

Rick

Entering the lobby, I can't help but think to myself just how ridiculously long it has been since I first stepped foot into Re-imagine Productions. I can't help it, because almost nothing has changed, and its age is quite literally on the wall.

And floor.

And probably concealed by the drop ceiling too.

There's a lot of age here.

The tile in the lobby is the same. The odd, stiff, carpet-texture wall paneling, cut into equilateral hexagons of altering hues of beige and a slightly darker beige behind the reception desk is the same, albeit dustier from the years of sameness. The studio logo hanging off the textured wall is the same. Geez, even Universal changes its logo every twenty years.

One thing that's changed for the better, Martha is now the senior receptionist at the front desk. About dang time!

"Good afternoon, Mr. Bennett," she greets me with her overly welcoming smile. I can never tell whether she's always so positive, or if it's just an act she's performed for decades. If it's the latter, then the studio has missed a trick in not casting her in any of its productions! In either case, she's always a pleasant sight any time I have to come here for another boring, or otherwise bothersome, meeting with another ignorant producer or director with whom I have conflicting creative views. Which is nearly all of them now.

"Good afternoon, Miss Crawford," I reply as pleasantly as possible. "And how many times have I asked you to call me Rick?"

"I'm waiting until you get the corner office for that," Martha responds with a playful wink.

I laugh. It doesn't sound genuine, but it is. Because I know Martha's joke is based in truth, and I appreciate it.

"You're here to see Mr. Morgan, correct?"

"Unfortunately, yes," I say.

Martha gives me a sympathetic pout and another encouraging wink before she begins typing on her keyboard and clicking her mouse several times, probably announcing my arrival in the company's internal (and no doubt archaic) calendaring system.

Abby was the one who arranged for the opportunity to repitch my script idea to Reimagine Productions. And, because setting up opportunities for me to pitch my creative ideas to major studios is my wife's love language, I couldn't refuse.

Even if it meant the meeting had to be with "pretty boy" Dylan Morgan.

God how I loathe that man. He absolutely reeks of pompousness, self-righteousness, and second-rate cologne. I know Abby doesn't care much for Morgan either, which begs the question why she arranged the meeting at all. Perhaps, at the time, she didn't know Morgan was going to be the one interested in pursuing this project. Perhaps she knew but didn't see it as a threat or issue in the grand plan. I doubt she thinks she can laud any power over Morgan to get him to do her bidding by producing her frail-egoed husband's project. Morgan isn't the kind of man to do another's bidding, even Abby's, despite the fact he owes her for much of his success. However, admitting that would mean he would have to be any kind of a decent human being, which Dylan Morgan certainly is not.

Why am I here again?

"Mr. Morgan is running late, but his secretary said you can wait for him outside his office," Martha says. "I'll get you a visitor's pass so you can take the elevator. Give me a moment."

I decide to look about the lobby a bit more while Martha prepares my badge, in hopes of trying to rekindle the memories of my first visit to the studio, the innocent, naive youth that I was back then. Apprehensive, clumsy, unable to form words in my mouth, yet still hoping the eloquence on my pages could sell my talent as a wordsmith. Though the walls and flooring are still the same, many of the pictures and posters have been noticeably updated. Along with the autographed headshots of the famous—and infamous—individuals who have contributed to the work produced by the studio, there is now a collection of behind-the-scenes photos from their more recent and popular productions. I particularly appreciate the photos featuring the studio's revolutionary Motion Capture stage. Animation has evolved immensely since I first pitched my early ideas for cartoon features and animation projects. I would bet money Abby thought the same thing when she put together this meeting for me. She's always supported my ideas and has faith in my words.

My wordsmithiness.

My wordsmithatude.

My wordsmithafication.

I pass the headshots and the production shots, and there it is, the one poster the studio will never remove from its lobby. The pride of the company, and *the* movie that solidified Reimagine Productions as one of the greats in the movie-making industry.

Grace Falls.

And there she is. My angel, standing with determination, soaking wet from a heavy rain, carrying her immense wings on her fragile back. The poster alone sold millions of copies. The copy in the lobby has signatures from all the major players, including Abby and Walter, and is proudly displayed in a gaudy, gilded frame adorned with a plaque, like a classic painting in a museum. I've never cared for the image. I think it grotesque. But then again, I was there when they shot that iconic scene, and I have my own emotional scars from that day, though not as deep as Abby's.

"Rick!" Martha calls from the receptionist desk.

I'm snapped out of my memory at the shock of Martha actually using my given name. I've wandered further down the hall than I realized.

"I got you a badge. Sorry about that. Mr. Morgan's on the seventh floor. His secretary will be up there to meet you."

I take the elevator to the seventh floor. I've correctly predicted that Morgan took Walter's old office. Walter's former office has the best view of the city next to the studio president's corner office, the office Martha is waiting for me to earn so that she can call me by my given name on the regular. Walter's old office is also the only office that is still an office, as the rest of the floor has been remodeled, and now sports the in vogue "open concept" work environment architectural magazines boast about with color photos of white and gray rooms.

I meet Morgan's secretary, Fortune, who asks me to take a seat just outside the office door. I make a bet with myself that he will make me wait half an hour after I sit down.

I lose my bet by three minutes.

Morgan opens his door and turns to me with the most obviously fake Hollywood producer smile I've ever seen. He's the personification of the stench of his cologne that day. I smile just to suppress my gag.

"Ricky! Long time no see, buddy," he greets with a strong two-fisted handshake. "So sorry to keep you waiting. Come in!"

Morgan leads me into his office. He's completely remodeled it from Walter's layout. I don't care much for it. His desk faces the office door as if to meet every visitor with a strong and, I imagine, overcompensating sense of intimidation. (Walter preferred an angle where he could see the door and the view of the city.) The polished gold name plate on his desk reads quite simply "Dylan Morgan: Producer." Flashy and to the point, I think to myself with a mental roll of my mind's eye.

Morgan invites me with a gesture of his right hand, which is adorned with a flashy class ring (which I assume he commissioned himself) to sit in one of the minimalist gray, stiff, padded chairs at the front of his desk, as he takes his seat in his garishly oversized leather chair, which consumes him like a throne made of dead cows. All the pictures on the shelves and walls are of him meeting celebrities or famous directors, most of whom are men. No pictures of his wife or son anywhere to be seen.

"How the hell are ya?" Morgan asks, leaning back in his chair, tapping his fingertips together, à la C. Montgomery Burns. "How long has it been since we chatted?"

"Well, not counting the parent/teacher mixer at our kids' school, I suppose it's been a while," I answer. Abby would have been proud of that passive aggressive retort.

"Ha! You're right! How's little Andy doing? He and Bruno are in the same class, you know."

"Yes." *I know, you ignorant subhuman,* I think. "And Andy's fine. Actually, my wife is visiting their class today for Career Day."

"Oh really? I thought Abby was flying up to Vancouver for a consulting gig or something."

"That's later in the afternoon. She didn't want to miss Career Day, since her trip would have had her miss her other windows of opportunity." I can't help but fidget in my seat. The foam in this chair must be made of plywood. Or particle board at least. They look like they're from IKEA. "So, I hear you're also doing a Career Day presentation?"

"Yes!" Morgan exclaims. "This Friday. Definitely looking forward to it. Can't wait to impress my boy's class, y'know? Show them all what success looks like."

Yes, because my far more successful wife isn't doing that now.

"Anyway," he continues, "let's talk about your story here. What did you call it? *The Boy Who Grew Antlers*?"

"Yes," I reply hoping to sound confident, but probably sounding apologetic for not coming up with a better title to my piece after so many years. "It's something I'd been working on for a while and was hoping to shop it around and see about getting a producer behind it. Abby said you may be interested in the project?"

"Well, that was generous of her to say." Morgan sits forward in his cow throne and puts his arms on his desk in front of him, holding his hands like some pretentious professor about to lecture a student about why they aren't fit to take Advanced European Lit. "I read it over the weekend and, truth is, it needs quite a bit of work."

In retrospect, I shouldn't have been surprised Morgan would say something like this to me. "Do you have any specific notes on what you think needs to be reworked?" I ask, trying to sound like some perfect mix of humble and completely aware of the precise state of my work.

"It needs more action," Morgan explained. "I mean, how're kids going to be entertained without action? What you have here seems to be, well, a lot of talking and inner dialogue."

"Well, I suppose I understand your point," I reply with some defensiveness. Maybe a little too much. "But it's supposed to be a tale about awkwardness and growing up and learning to deal with others. It's not really a story meant for lots of action."

"Don't get me wrong," Morgan continues, playing the "I'm on your side" card worse than an accident lawyer on their own commercial, "I'm digging the moral angle, but you have to keep kids' attention if you want them to learn anything, right? What gets their attention? Action!"

Just then, I feel my phone buzz in my pocket. As I reach for it, I happen to notice Morgan glancing at his phone at the same time. It, too, seems to be buzzing. I look at the screen and see a message from Andy's school and a request to call back. I stand up from my seat to excuse myself. "I'm sorry, it's from Andy's teacher. I need to take this."

"All good," Morgan says, standing up from his cow throne (which suddenly gives me an idea for a new retail outlet). "I'll have Fortune send you my detailed notes."

I wasn't expecting him to completely shut down the meeting, but I welcome the reprieve from his company all the same.

"Think you could get me a rewrite by this Thursday?"

"Thursday?" I ask, stunned. I catch the words in my throat before I say anything I'll regret later and, instead, say what I would have preferred not to: "Sure, I'll do what I can. Thanks again."

"No worries." Morgan escorts me out of his office, all but pushing me toward the door. "I look forward to your rewrites."

I cross the glorious threshold, back into the minimalist paradise of glass desks and cruelty-free upholstery.

"Fortune," Morgan says, peeking just barely out of his office doorway, "make sure he gets a La Croix on his way out."

"Yes, sir," she replies timidly.

Morgan walks back into his office and shuts the door rather callously. Fortune and I both close our eyes and twitch at the sound.

"I don't need a drink," I immediately and kindly tell Fortune. "Thanks anyways."

"No problem, Mr. Bennett," she says with some relief. "Truth is, I don't know where all the drinks are. I only started last week."

I smile and bid her a pleasant farewell. I take the elevator back down to the lobby, return my badge to Martha, say my farewells, get my last few winks, and step outside into the building's front courtyard to make my call.

"Hi, this is Rick Bennett, Andrew's father. I got a message that I should call back? ... Oh, is everything all right? ... I see. ... Yes, I'll be there to pick him up. Thanks for letting me know. ... Yes, of course. I'll be there shortly. Take care."

While I appreciate the excuse to end my meeting with Dylan Morgan early, this is not the escape I hoped for.

Andy

Dad is angry at me. Very angry. The car ride home is very quiet, and Dad isn't usually this quiet.

"So, who started the fight, you or Bruno?" he finally asks me.

I can't answer right away. I'm too afraid.

"Mrs. Perkins said it may've started with something Bruno said during Mom's Career Day talk?"

"Bruno said Mom was ugly," I say, staring at my lap. "Well, he said that his dad said she was ugly. But Mom said that he should tell his dad that he was cuter than his dad, and that made everyone laugh."

"What happened next?" Dad asks.

"Then, after lunch, Bruno pushed me in the hall and said

Mom made fun of him and that I had to apologize. I didn't want to apologize, so I pushed him back. Then we started to fight."

Dad lets out a big sigh and shakes his head. I can see him say the word "dammit" to himself. I'm not allowed to point out when Mom or Dad cuss in front of me.

Then Dad asks, "Did you get hurt bad?"

I shake my head.

"Did Bruno get hurt?"

"I don't think so," I say quietly.

"You know I'm going to have to tell your mother about this," Dad says, very seriously.

"Please don't tell Mom!" I beg. Making Dad angry is bad, but making Mom angry is even worse.

"She'll have to be told," Dad replies. "But," he continues, "we can wait until tomorrow."

I let out a sigh of relief.

"I am still grounding you, though," Dad says. "Starting when we get home, no computer, no TV, and no video games until your mother gets home."

"But—"

"Nope."

We drive up and into our super long driveway and pull into the garage. I can't really explain it, since all the cars are technically here, but it always feels weird to pull up to the house when Mom isn't home. Maybe it's because when Mom isn't home, the house is always darker.

I drop my stuff off at the bench in the foyer and start to run up to my room when Dad calls me.

"You're doing your homework in my office so I can make sure you're not using your computer," Dad says sternly.

I trudge back down the stairs, grab my backpack, and go to Dad's downstairs office. He has a table in the corner of his office where I can do my homework while he works on his writing. He says I'm always invited to write or draw in his office any time I want, whether he's working or not, but I only ever do when I'm in trouble.

I pull out my take-home worksheets and a pencil while Dad orders pizza for dinner.

On the wall next to his desk, Dad has a corkboard with the words "Ideas and Inspiration" spelled out in letters cut out of different kinds of wood just above it. He usually uses the board to post pictures or articles or anything that's related to something he's trying to write, like pictures of cities in different countries or different mountains or beaches. One time, he had an article about the International Space Station with a really neat picture of it in space. I think he must've been writing a story about space travel or something. I don't remember.

Today, the board is almost completely covered with pictures of deer. Just deer. Some are young deer (Fawns, I guess? Like Bambi?) and others are big deer with big antlers. I count seventeen different deer on the board. I wondered what they are all for?

Dad comes back into his office, and I quickly go back to my table to do my worksheets, doing my best not to look up at Dad since I know he's watching me.

Dad sits down at his desk and quietly starts clicking and typing on his iMac. He has one of those really thin Apple keyboards that sounds like he's clicking a really quiet pen or something every time he types. I've seen Dad get so focused on his writing that he can't tell what else is going on around him. One time, the smoke alarm went off when Mom burned cookies she was baking, and when she went to apologize for the noise, Dad said he didn't even notice. It looks like Dad is going to be that kind of focused again. I can tell by his eyebrows. They look very straight and sharp.

I must've really made him angry.

I finish all my worksheets pretty quickly and put them back in my backpack. Dad doesn't notice. I just sit at the table quietly and play with my pencils, not really knowing what to say or do. If Dad's really angry, I don't want to bother him. Dad's not really mean when he's angry, but he gets really, really sad and really, really serious. Usually, Dad likes to tell stories and jokes and hear about my day. When he's sad or angry or serious, he's extra quiet, and it makes me feel uncomfortable. I just wait at the table rolling and clicking my pencils until the pizza arrives.

Normally when Mom is out of town and Dad orders pizza, we will sit in the living room and watch movies or TV shows I'm allowed to watch when Mom's home. Tonight, Dad makes us eat in the dining room where we can't even see the TV.

We're eating our pizza and it's still extra quiet. Dad is looking at his plate and his eyebrows are still straight. I must've really, *really* made him mad.

I don't like the quiet anymore, so I ask, "Why do you have all those pictures of deer on your idea board?"

Dad looks up at me, and his eyebrows relax and he smiles. Maybe he's not really, really mad at me.

"It's a story I'm working on called *The Boy Who Grew Ant-lers*," he answers. "It's about a kid who deals with his bully by growing antlers. I came up with this idea a long time ago—before you were born, in fact. Mom found me an opportunity to try and get it produced, so I'm working on it again now. Did you know antlers are an indicator of how mature a buck is?"

"No," I say. I wait for Dad to continue.

Dad looks at me like he's waiting for *me* to continue. I take a bite of my pizza. Dad just sighs. What did I do wrong this time?

"So, I'm probably going to be working most of tonight," Dad then says. "Why don't you grab one of your sketchbooks and pencils and do some drawing in my office."

I don't really like the idea of drawing in Dad's office tonight. I would rather go to bed, but it's still too early for bedtime, and Dad would think I'm just trying to get away and do something that will break his rules.

"I guess," I say. Maybe hanging out with Dad won't be that bad. At least if I'm in the same room as him, I can make sure he doesn't call Mom.

After dinner, I bring my sketchbook and pencils from my room and set myself up at my table in Dad's office again. Dad suggests I pick a few of the pictures of deer off his board and try to draw a picture of a boy with antlers for fun. He says it might help him with his project. I don't actually like that idea. I kinda don't feel like helping Dad with his project—I'm still kinda mad at him for grounding me.

If I *have* to draw a picture of a boy with antlers for Dad's story, I'll draw myself as the boy with antlers. And I'll draw myself with the biggest and strongest antlers I can. Bigger than any other boy possibly could have. I want antlers so big that, if Bruno or any other kid saw them, they would be too scared to tease me.

They would be so big and scary, no one would want to fight me. Maybe even antlers so big Dad wouldn't bother me or ground me. And Mom wouldn't have to protect me from Bruno with stupid comments.

I keep thinking about the fight I had with Bruno today. I replay the fight over and over again in my head. First Bruno said I had to apologize because Mom embarrassed him in front of everyone. I said I didn't have to apologize. He yelled at me, and then he pushed me first. I yelled at him and pushed him back. Then we started pushing each other and yelling at each other until Mrs. Perkins came and stopped the fight and brought us to Mr. Foldger's office. Mr. Foldger sat us down in his office and kept telling us that fighting was bad and that they were calling our parents to pick us up. I got scared and upset because I knew Dad was going to be mad at me.

Bruno just shrugged and said, "Whatever," and that made me even more mad. But I was more scared than mad, and I didn't say anything.

I think about all this over and over again while I'm drawing. The more I remember the fight, the bigger my antlers get in my picture.

And the more I remember the fight, the angrier and angrier I get at Bruno—angrier than I was when we were actually fighting. How could he say I had to apologize? I didn't do anything!

And who was his dad to say Mom was ugly? Who says that about someone's mom anyway?

And why would he say that to my mom in front of everyone? Was he trying to embarrass me? Was he jealous or something? Who cares! Me and my antlers are gonna—

"Andy, it's 9:00," Dad says.

He surprises me and I jump a little. I can't believe I've been drawing for so long! Was Dad writing all that time too? I put my pencil down. Wow, my hand actually hurts. I must have been drawing super hard too!

Dad walks me upstairs to my room. While I brush my teeth in my bathroom, Dad goes into my room and takes the power cord from my computer to make sure I don't turn it on after he goes to bed. I'm so mad.

Dad watches me get into my bed and turns off the light in my room. I turn over in bed and face away from the door as Dad says, "Good night."

I don't say anything back. I hear the door shut a second later.

I lie in my bed, but I'm not tired. I still can't stop thinking about today. Everyone came to class, even people who shouldn't have been there, and watched Bruno make fun of my mom. Then Bruno started the fight with me. Why? I didn't want to fight! I mean, I wanted to punch him in the face for saying that stuff to Mom, but still, I didn't start the fight!

Then Bruno pushed me into the lockers. He pushed me first! I only pushed him because he pushed me! Then I think about my drawing. If we both had antlers, I could push him even harder! We would fight like bucks, but I would win! I would win because I had the bigger antlers! And when I would tell Dad my story, he would say that my idea was way better than his, and he could write an even better script! All I'd have to do is get antlers and I could beat Bruno in a fight!

I think about it so much I even dream about growing antlers! In my dream, I'm with Bruno in the school hallway. He pushes me into the lockers, but this time I'm ready. I can feel something sticking out of the top of my head. Two things. I reach up to feel what they are. They feel hard and pointy, but not sharp. I have so many antlers I can't even count them all.

I can't believe it! I have antlers!

I bend my head down and charge at Bruno. Bruno screams and starts running away. I run after him. I'm getting closer. I'm going to get him!

Then, just as I'm about to run into Bruno, I bolt out of bed. It's morning.

Dangit! Even in my dreams I can't get him.

I look at my clock. It's twenty minutes before my alarm's supposed to go off. Ugh.

I lay back down on my pillow. Huh. My pillow feels...weird. Like something's pushing on the top of my head. I sit up and look at my pillow. Huh. Nothing's there. I put my head down again. Still feels weird. I sit up again. There's still nothing on my pillow. Maybe there's something stuck to my head?

I reached up to touch my head, and—

Wait. What's this? There *is* something stuck to my head. Two somethings. I push on them a little. Ow! It feels like something's pulling on the skin over my skull. Man, these must be really stuck, whatever they are. Did I get glue in my hair, and when I was sleeping roll into something that's stuck on my head? Oh man, if I got something stuck in my hair and I have to get my hair cut, Dad and Mom are going to kill me.

I get out of bed and walk to the bathroom. I gotta see what this is and see if I can get it unstuck before Dad gets up. I turn on the bathroom light. I look in the mirror.

No...

No way...

How...?

Did the dream do this? Was it because of everything I was thinking about last night?

I don't know what I did or how I did it, but somehow, last night, I started growing antlers!

2

〜

The Boy Who Grew Antlers

Andy

Antlers?

Seriously?

What the heck?

I have so many more questions. Mostly, how?

How am I growing antlers? How am I going to get rid of them?

And if I can't get rid of them, how am I supposed to hide them from Dad?

Wait, is this what Mom was talking about yesterday in class? Is this...a transformation?

Did I just grow extra parts on my body?

I look closely at the—*my*—antlers. They're kinda thick at the base and almost straight up from my head. They're rounded at the top, not sharp. The longer one on the left curls forward where the shorter one on the right is straight. I carefully run my fingers over them. They're almost the same color as my hair and are actually kinda soft, like I have hair glued to the outside of bone or something. Ugh, gross. I need to think of a better way to describe that.

I run back to my room and close the door. *Oh man, I hope that wasn't too loud. I can't wake up Dad!* I open my closet and tear through my clothes. I need to find something to hide these things! If Dad sees these things on my head, he'll kill me, or worse—call Mom.

I have to think. What do I do? I need a way to look up how to get rid of these without Dad finding out. If Mom were here, she'd know. She knows how to get rid of her transformations. Does she have any books? I can't remember. Gramma might have books, but then I'd have to call her, and I'd have to tell her what happened, and I don't know that I can trust Gramma not to call Mom. I mean, about this. Gramma hides stuff we do all the time from Mom.

But this isn't the same as having ice cream for dinner. This is antlers! On my head!

I need the internet. But Dad took my power cord. Where can I get on the internet? That's it! The school library! I need to get out of the house and get to school without Dad seeing me. If I can get to school, I can use one of the computers in the library and look up what to do to ungrow my antlers.

I dig through my closet. I gotta have a hat or something in here. Anything that will fit over my head. Dangit, all I have are a couple baseball caps and a small beanie. None of these will cover these things! I pull out a hoodie. Maybe the hood will cover my head, at least so I can get downstairs and look through the coat closet. I know we have tons of hats there.

The hood works. Well, sorta. I pull it over my forehead, but it still looks like I have something poking up through the top of my head. It'll have to do.

I put on my soft slippers and carefully, *carefully* creep down. I put my foot on the first step. Then the second. Then...*uuuuurk.* I freeze. Was that too loud? I listen. I don't hear Dad. I take the next step. Then the next. Then...*uuuuurk.* Really? Since when have our stairs been this creaky? I listen again. I don't think I hear anything. I look down at the remaining steps. I take a breath and hold it. Then...

urk urk urk urk urk urk

I'm at the bottom. I listen. Is that some rustling? Or is that the steps moving back into place?

Since when is our house so noisy?!

I quietly walk to the foyer. Finally, the coat closet. I listen. I don't hear any sound from upstairs. Dad must not have heard me! I open the door and find the basket of scarves, hats, and gloves. There has to be something in there I could wear over my—

"Andy?"

I freeze. What the heck? Dad's right behind me! Where did he come from? How did he get downstairs without me hearing him?

I reach my hand down into the basket and grab the first hat I can find and quickly pull it over my head. I turn around to face Dad.

"Morning!" I say, smiling innocently...I hope.

"Hey," Dad says. He frowns and raises and eyebrow. Oh no...oh no... "Are you cold or something?" he asks.

Maybe he doesn't see them. "Um, yes," I answer. "I think I left my window open last night or something."

"Are you feeling sick or anything?" Dad asks.

"Um...no," I say. Dad looks suspicious. Oh man, should I have said, yes, I do feel sick?

"Okay..." Dad's definitely not convinced. He's still looking at me weird.

"So...I'm going to go get dressed now," I say.

"Alright," Dad says, still looking suspicious. "Would you like me to drive you in today, or are you going to take the bus?"

"Um...maybe I can walk today?" I say.

"Andy, you know you can't walk," Dad says, a little frustrated. Oh no, please don't get mad at me. Not this morning.

"We're too far away from your school to walk. Look, if you're concerned about dealing with Bruno on the bus, I can drive you. I don't mind. But you're not walking. Especially if you think you might be unwell."

"Um...yeah. No. Yeah. I'll, um...I'll get dressed, and then you can drive me?"

Dad looks at me for another long second. "Okay," he says. "Are you planning on wearing your mother's hat to school too?"

Mom's hat? What hat did I pull from the basket? "Um...yes?" I say. "I mean, only until I get dressed. Then I'll find my hat."

"Alright," Dad says. He's still suspicious. What am I saying, of course he's suspicious. I'm wearing Mom's winter hat!! "Go get dressed and come down to the kitchen for breakfast when you're done."

"Thanks!" I bolt up the stairs as fast as I can, and go back into my room, slamming the door behind me. I tear the hat off my head. Which one did I grab? Oh man, it's Mom's fluffy pink and purple butterfly hat, probably the girliest hat she owns. Ugh.

I pull out a random T-shirt and pants and put my hoodie back on. I put Mom's hat back on and pull my hood all the way over it. Well, as far over it as it can go. Mom's hat is actually covering the antlers really well. But I totally can't wear this to school! I don't want the attention.

I run back downstairs to the coat closet. I think I have a hat kinda like this, only less purple butterfly-y. Maybe that'll cover my antlers alright.

I hear Dad call out from the kitchen, "Andy, come and have your breakfast."

"In a sec!" I call back. Where's that dang hat?

"Now, Andy," Dad says.

Ugh. If I don't do what Dad says, he's gonna call Mom. I just have to eat quickly, then I can go back to looking for my hat. Mom's hat is doing a good job of covering my antlers, and my hood is doing an okay job of covering Mom's hat. Maybe it won't be a big deal. I mean, Dad probably doesn't care if I wear a girl's hat.

I go to the kitchen and sit at the counter. I try not to look at Dad.

"What cereal do you want for breakfast?" he asks.

"Frosted Flakes," I say.

Dad pours me a bowl of cereal with milk and places it in front of me. I just keep staring at the counter. Oh man. This is totally not going to work. Dad's already totally too suspicious. He's going to ask what I'm doing, and I won't be able to explain. What am I going to do?

Great, now my head is itchy. I reach up to scratch my head but catch myself just before I do. I can't risk accidentally pushing the hat off. Ugh! This is so uncomfortable!

"Bud, are you sure you're not feeling sick?" Dad asks.

"Nah," I reply quickly, shoveling cereal into my mouth. "Like I said, my head is cold is all." I hold tightly onto my bowl and spoon. Maybe this will help keep me from scratching my head. I keep shoveling cereal into my mouth, eating as quickly as I can.

"Nothing you want to talk about?" Dad asks. "Look, I'm sorry about your punishment last night. I promise I haven't told Mom anything yet, but I'm probably going to have to tell her when I talk to her today. You understand that, right?"

"Yep," I say, still shoveling more cereal into my mouth and staring at the counter. Anything I can do to keep from scratching my head and get back to the coat closet to find my hat.

"Are you sure?" Dad asks.

"Uh huh," I say. Two more bits.

Dad sighs. He's frustrated. "Alright. Can you be ready in fifteen minutes? I'll drive you to school."

Last bite. "Yep. Thanks Dad!" I eat the last bite of cereal and push the stool out from under the bar. Gotta get to the closet.

"Sink!" Dad calls out.

Ugh! Can't disobey Dad. I grab my bowl and spoon and drop them in the sink. They clang loudly, maybe a little more than I meant. I start heading back to the closet. I just wanted to get away from Dad so badly.

"Andy!"

"What?" I shout back.

Oh no...

I just talked back to Dad.

He's going to—

"Andrew William Bennett, what is wrong with you today?"

—say my full name and scold me.

"Look, I'm sorry you're upset that you're grounded, but you brought this on yourself. It's one thing to lose your temper with some kid at school. It's another to lose your temper with your father."

This is weird. Dad's usually the calm one. Mom's usually the one to yell at me if I'm really in trouble. I mean, I did just talk back to him, but usually he takes a breath and says my name calmly and asks what I did wrong, and we talk about how to act differently. He's not usually this mad.

Did I really do all this to him? I didn't mean to if I did.

Dad lets out a huge sigh and rubs the bridge of his nose. "Be back here in fifteen minutes with all your stuff. Don't be tardy."

"Okay," I say quietly. I walk out of the kitchen regularly; I don't run away. Dad is super upset. I've never seen him so angry or frustrated with anything. Now I feel really bad. But I don't know what to do. I can't tell him about my antlers now. If I do, he's going to be mondo upset!

I pass Dad's office on the way back to the coat closet. The light's still on over his desk. Wait, was he in his office all night? Is that why I didn't hear him come downstairs? Because he was downstairs the whole time?

I pull the basket of hats out of the closet so I can see everything in the light. Ahh, there's the hat I'm looking for, my thick gray knit beanie, just as loose and soft as Mom's hat, but without the purple butterflies. No offense, Mom, but your hat looks better on you.

I run into the downstairs bathroom and close the door. I unknot my hoodie drawstring and take off Mom's hat. Finally, I scratch the top of my head in the space between my antlers. Man, this feels so weird. I can feel them moving on top of my head. It doesn't hurt, it just feels...weird. I put my hat on over my antlers. Much better. The hat's stiff enough on top that it's not obvious that it's covering anything. It just looks like it's sitting on top of my head. That should work for today. It has to if I want to use the library and figure out how to get rid of these things.

I come back out to the foyer, put on my shoes, grab my book-bag, and wait for Dad. I feel so much better now. I'm wearing my hat and my head isn't itchy anymore. Dad comes downstairs a few minutes later, dressed and ready to go. He looks at me concerned and a little confused. Is the hat not working?

"Can I go into your room today and check your windows?" he asks. "If it really is that cold, I want to see if we need to re-caulk your windows or something. I don't want you getting sick."

"Sure," I say quietly.

Maybe Dad's more worried than suspicious. Huh, I wonder which is better for my current situation.

The ride to school is more quiet and awkward than the ride home yesterday. I really can't tell what Dad's thinking, and I don't want to ask. The less he pays attention to me, the better chance he won't see my head and suspect anything. So I stay quiet the whole time.

We pull into the parking lot, and I quickly get out of the car. I start to walk away when Dad calls out to me through the passenger window.

"Andy!"

I turn back around and look at him.

"Listen," he says, "I don't know what happened this morning, but I want you to know that that wasn't all your fault, okay? I didn't get a whole lot of sleep last night, and I might be a little on edge. So, for my part, I just wanted to say I'm sorry."

Wow. Dad was up all night. Oh man, I hope everything's okay with his project. I don't know what I should say, so I just nod. I do feel a little better that Dad isn't as mad at me, but I still don't want to spend much more time talking to him either. I'll make it up to him later. I promise.

"Would you like me to pick you up after school, or do you want to take the bus?" he asks.

"Um...I can take the bus," I say, though I'm thinking I'll actually walk home instead. I don't like lying to Dad and breaking his rules, but I don't have a choice. Not if I still have these antlers.

"Alright," Dad says, smiling. "Have a good day, buddy. Love you."

"Yeah," I say. "Thanks, Dad."

I turn and walk over to stand in my class line to wait to enter school. Dad pulls out of the parking lot and drives away.

Alright. Gotta figure out how I'm going to get through today. I've already decided I'm going to walk home after school. No way am I taking the bus or having Dad pick me up. Besides, it sounds like Dad had a rough night anyway. If Miss Perkins asks why I'm wearing a hat, I'll tell her it was cold in my room last night, and my dad wanted me to wear my hat, in case I'm getting sick. She's usually cool with answers like that. Then, I'll ask if, instead of going to recess, I can go to the library, since I might not be feeling well from the cold. Maybe I should pretend to cough a little. Mom always says it's the little things that sell a performance.

Then, when I get to the library I have to look up how to fix this and ungrow my antlers. Or really, transformations. I used to listen to Mom and Gramma talk about their transformations all the time. I remember they said that the Muse had to want to change, and it was always their decision—no one can make a transformation unless they wanted it. But I always thought a transformation could only happen with a Muse *and* a Creator. So how did I make a transformation without a Creator? That will be the first thing I look up when I get to a computer.

I remember Mom also said transformations don't last very long, maybe even only a day. But wait, didn't she say she could keep her transformations for almost a week sometimes if she had to? I definitely can't let that happen. That's probably something else I should look up, so I make sure I *don't* do that.

The morning bell rings, and we're all let into the school building. I can't look at anyone, not even my teacher. If I look at them, they might want to talk to me.

I pull the hood over my hat and stare at my feet as I walk into my classroom. I take my seat at my desk and immediately put my head down. Hey, maybe this will also make it look like I'm sick. Can't look too sick, though. I don't want them calling Dad to pick me up before I can get to the library.

I wonder...maybe if I just think really hard, they'll go away. Maybe if I think really hard, right now, while my head's down, they'll even go away before class starts. It's worth a shot!

I start repeating to myself, *go away...go away...go away...*

"Can't show your face in class, huh, Mommy's Boy?"

Ugh. That voice. Bruno.

"Dude, why're you hiding your ugly face? Afraid your ugly Mommy might see you cry?"

Go away...go away...

"My dad says, not only is your mommy ugly, she's not a good actress either."

Shut up, Bruno! *Go away...go away...*

"He said she had to leave acting because she was so bad and it's all because she married your dad and had you for a son."

Go away...go away...

"My dad also said—"

"Your dad is a jerk!" I can't take it anymore. I just scream at him while my head is down. "Your dad is a jerk, and you're a bigger jerk."

"My dad said you're weak and that's why you got in trouble for getting into a fight."

"You got in trouble too!"

"Nope. Dad was proud of me. And I'm not in trouble."

What?

Bruno's *not* in trouble?

While I was grounded and forced to think about what I did wrong yesterday, Bruno was probably at home playing video games, watching TV, and browsing the internet on his computer.

While I was sitting at home angry because I *didn't* start the fight, Bruno was at home being told he did a good job *for* starting it.

Why am I in trouble and he's not? How is that fair?!

Just then...oh no. I think I feel my hat switch on my head.

Oh no…is something happening with my antlers? Oh no. If anyone sees…

I quickly lift my head up and barely miss Bruno's chin. He's standing over me with his hands holding both sides of my desk. I look around. The whole class is watching Bruno taunt me. Why isn't anyone helping? I open my mouth to yell back at him again, but Mrs. Perkins comes into the room.

"What's going on here?" she demands. "Mr. Morgan, take your seat immediately!"

"Whatever," he says.

Mrs. Perkins scowls at him but doesn't say anything. Again, he's not being punished.

I hear him whisper as he walks away, "Mommy's Boy."

"Mr. Bennett," she says before I can say anything, "please remove your hood and sit up at your desk."

I carefully lower my hood.

"And your hat."

"Um…" I start. "I woke up with a cold head this morning, so my dad said I could wear this hat today." I hear the kids in my class laughing quietly and whispering to each other. Oh no. It's not going to work. She's going to make me take off my hat.

Please let me keep it on.

Please let me keep it on.

"Fine," Mrs. Perkins finally says. "As long as I can see your eyes and forehead."

"Yes, ma'am."

I am soooooo relieved. I adjust the hat a little so it's not quite covering my forehead and pull some of my hair out so it's not all stuffed under the hat. Now maybe it doesn't look like I'm trying to hide anything. *Little things sell the performance, right, Mom?*

The school day starts normally with morning announcements. Afterward, Mrs. Perkins reminds the class that we have another Career Day visit today. Jayme Murdoch's dad, who is a vet at the zoo, is going to be visiting us today. Since Dr. Murdoch is visiting this afternoon, maybe I'll ask to skip out and go to the library then instead of recess. I could make an excuse and say the noise or the air-conditioning is giving me a headache. Plus, I could probably stay longer, since the Career Day visits are usually longer than recess. Yes, this could totally work!

All I have to do was get through the morning and lunch. I can do this. I think I can do this.

* * *

The morning is taking forever. Ahhhhhhhhh!

I keep watching the clock, waiting for it to hit read 11:25, the start of lunch. But it's only 9:25. It was 9:25, like, an hour ago!

9:25, we switch from language arts to math. Ugh. Math's going to be even more of a drag. We're learning times tables and how to multiply. I already know how to multiply!

10:25, we switched from math to science, which was pushed to the morning because of Career Day. Science is even worse. It's like math and vocabulary combined. And I hate vocabulary! Uuuuuugh.

My head starts to itch again. I grip my pencil harder. Can't touch my head...Can't touch my head...

I look up just as the clock turns to 11:00. Only twenty-five more minutes of talking about plant cells. I can do this. I think I can do this.

I start doodling in the margins of my notebook instead of listening to Mrs. Perkins. I'm doodling more antlers. I can't think of anything else to draw or even really to do. Anything to make time go faster. I promise I'll read up on what I missed later. Or at least I will try to. Right now, I have more important things to deal with.

RIIIIIIIING

Finally! The lunch bell! Lunch will go by fast. I usually draw in my sketchbook, anyway, while I eat. And no one usually bothers me, so no worries about people wondering if there's something on my head. Everyone thinks I just had a cold night.

And my head stopped being itchy too! Thank goodness!

We all leave the classroom, and I go to my locker to get the lunch Dad packed for me, along with my sketchbook from my bookbag. This will be great. Just gotta get through lunch, then recess. I can do this. I think I can do this.

I shut the door to my locker when someone tugs on my hood.

"Hey!"

Ugh. That voice. *Go away...go away...*

"Hey! Don't ignore me, Mommy's Boy!"

Go away. Go away!

"Hey! I'm talking to you, loser!"

Then I feel another tug. This time on my head.

No. Not the hat!

"Hey! Stop ignoring me!"

Bruno pulls on the back of my hat again. I feel the hat get caught on my antlers as he pulls my head back.

No! Please don't pull my hat off!

I grab at my hat and hold it tight. Did he...see them? He's laughing.

I feel myself getting angrier.

"What's going on with your hat, man?" Bruno asks. "Is there something on your head? Did you glue something to your head or something? What are you trying to hide?"

I freeze. I'm furious. I can't talk. I feel my fingernails pressing my palms as I gripped my hat tighter. Then...

They're growing. I feel them growing! I don't know what to do!

"Go away!" I scream. I don't know if I'm screaming at Bruno or screaming at my antlers, but I had to scream something.

I turn around and face Bruno. He just looks at me, confused. Then starts laughing again.

"What?" he says.

"Go away! Leave me alone!"

Before I realize it, I'm running down the hall. I don't know who I'm passing or what people are yelling at me. I just need to get out of here. I don't care if I'm pushing a kid into a locker. I don't care if I'm pushing a teacher into a wall. I don't even care if I push the principal.

I don't care if I get suspended. I don't care if I get expelled. I don't care if my parents ground me for life and never speak to me ever again. I don't care.

I just have to get out of this building. I have to get out of here before Bruno or anyone sees them. Sees me. Sees my antlers.

I slam into one of the side exit doors and run as fast as I can across the sports fields, past the teacher's parking lot, onto the sidewalk and down the street. I don't care if anyone's following me, I'm just going to keep running.

I can feel them growing. They've pushed the hat completely off my head. I don't even know if my hat is still on them. All I know is I have to get away.

I have to get away.

I run to Jordan Park. I'm very familiar with this park. This has the playground Mom and Dad would bring me to when I was very little. This is where Mom would take me when I was having a tantrum and needed to run off some steam. This is where Dad brought me to teach me how to climb trees. I like this place. I should be safe here.

I run through the park to the woods in the back. There. Our favorite tree. Back when Dad was teaching me how to climb, I was only allowed to climb just above Dad's head. Now, I'm going to climb as high above the ground as I possibly can. I have to get away. I have to hide.

I start climbing. I climb and climb and climb. I don't stop. I don't want to stop. All I can think about is running and hiding.

Ouch! I can feel my antlers getting caught on the branches! I shake my head to get loose and keep climbing. The scratching sound of the leaves and branches is loud in my ears. It's the only thing I can hear. My hat gets caught on a branch along the way. I just leave it in the tree. I can't turn back. I have to keep climbing. I have to get away.

Eventually, I'm high enough in the tree that the branches are too thin to support me. This is the highest I've ever climbed in any tree. I try to look around, but my antlers are caught in the branches again. It hurts, and I try to shake my head, but I can't.

I'm stuck! The scratching leaves are even louder now. I want to escape, but I can't. I can't get my head loose!

I can't do this.

I just start to cry. I don't know what to do. I'm in so much trouble. I'm stuck in a tree. And nobody knows where I—

"Andy?"

I look around to find where the voice is coming from.

"Andy, is that you up there?"

I can't climb down. I can't even look down and see who's calling me. And the scratch leaves and branches get louder and louder when I move my head that I can barely hear who's calling me. I'm in so much trouble.

"Andy, I'm coming up to get you, okay?"

I hear rustling below me as someone starts climbing my tree. I can't look. I just can't look. I stop shaking my head and just close my eyes tight. Whoever this is, they're going to see my antlers. They're going to be angry. Or scared. They're going to call the police, who are going to call my dad. And Dad's going to tell Mom. And they're both going to be angry with me. Furious with me. Because I did a transformation that I didn't mean to do. Just like Mom told me never to do because it's too dangerous. And then everyone at school is going to find out. And Bruno's going to find out. And he's going to use it to taunt me and make fun of me and bully me until the day I die.

I just want to be left alone. *Just leave me alone!*

I feel a hand gently grab my thigh. "Andy?"

Wait, I *do* know that voice. I open my eyes.

"Dad?"

"Hey, buddy," Dad says. He's climbed up the tree almost as

high as me. He doesn't sound angry at all. "Are you okay? Are you hurt?"

I try to answer, but I can't. I start crying harder. Dad climbs up a little higher. I feel him gently take my hand. I take my other hand and point to my head. "I...I didn't mean to. I'm sorry."

Dad doesn't say anything. I can't see Dad's face. My eyes are too filled with tears to see clearly.

Then, I hear him say very gently and very quietly, "Andy, are those...antlers?"

3

The Boy Who Called for Help

Rick

With a bit of misdirection, quick footwork, and a lot of branches and leaves, Andy and I manage to get out of the tree and into my car.

The school had called me and explained that Andy had been verbally attacked by another student at the start of lunch and ran out of the building and off campus "before anyone could stop him." I told the school I would immediately check the familiar spots and that we would be in touch. I'll have words with the administration later about their lack of reactive or even preventative action to protect my son.

Oh, I'm livid.

I knew immediately where to check first. Whenever Andy gets upset, the first thing he'll do is look for a tree to climb. His affinity for climbing trees was so prevalent we had to trim all the lowest limbs in the trees bordering our yard to keep him from climbing them when he got in trouble. There's one tree between the school and the house he could still climb, and sure enough, that's where I found him. Abby would be proud that I know our son so well.

Of course, that will be after she murders the both of us after learning our son somehow grew antlers.

I think I'll let Andy decompress before he and I have a talk. He immediately retreats to the living room couch and buries his face in a cushion. I retreat to my office and close the door. I can feel a stress headache coming on. I call Andy's school to let them know I was able to find him unharmed and that he will probably be missing school tomorrow. They don't give me any guff. Good. I have enough to deal with at the moment.

I collapse into my desk chair and let out a deep breath. What am I going to do? As terrified as Andy is of his mother finding out what's happened, I'm just as petrified. From the moment Abby and I met, to the moment I realized she was in love with me, too, I feared her. She was so perfect and was just untouchable to the "common folk" like myself. She was one of the most revered movie stars in the world! Certainly one of the most beautiful. When the reality finally sunk in that she genuinely wanted to be with me, I feared losing her. Somehow, I'd been blessed with this amazing treasure, and I vowed to her I would do everything in my power to preserve this and never take it for granted.

Then we had Andy, and ever since, I've feared losing both of them. From the instant he was born, he became our world. His happiness and safety is our happiness. What hurts him crushes us twice as much. Any time he's in pain—a skinned knee, a hurt feeling, a disappointment of any kind—there's an ache in our hearts.

Whatever Andy is going through right now, it feels like a dagger to my heart. I yelled at him this morning, unaware that he was dealing with something so unknown, so frightening, surely it made his day worse.

I glance at my corkboard, and it dawns on me: I did this. I put the idea into his mind.

I gave him antlers.

This cursed story!

First things first. My son has grown antlers. We don't know how, and we'll figure that out later. Right now, I need to find my son help.

And I need to find it without his mother finding out.

Andy

I hate crying. It always gives me a headache. How bad is a headache going to be with these stupid antlers on my head? Still, screaming into the cushions is kinda helping.

After screaming a bunch into the couch cushion, I lift my head and try to sit up straight. Oh man, my head feels so wobbly, like trying to balance two heavy brooms, but they're also stuck to my skin. I wonder what they look like now. I mean, I know they're bigger than they were this morning.

I stand up from the couch and...

Whoa...

Whoa...

Oh man, it's hard to balance with these things! I feel like I'm going to topple over. I put my feet further apart. Maybe that will help me balance.

I lean a little forward. Then backward. Then...

I'm good!

Carefully, I take a step.

Whoa...I'm good!

Another step...still good.

Step. Step. Step. Whoa!

Step. Step. Yes! I make it to the bathroom.

I turn on the light and look in the mirror and...wow. They're huge! Both are now curled out and then back in again. They kinda looked like a bunch of thumbs and forefingers sticking up. They look like antlers on antlers now.

I reach up and carefully grab them, one in each hand. They're hard. Very hard. Almost like...bone, maybe? I dig my nails into them a little to see if I can feel something, like a poke or a prick. Nothing. I pull on them a little. Eww. It's like all the skin on the top of my head moved a little. It doesn't hurt but it's...weird...in a not good way.

Suddenly, Dad appears in the bathroom doorway. He sees me trying to move my antlers around. I think he's trying not to laugh. "You feeling a little better, bud?" he asks.

"I'm...not sure," I say. "These are really freaky. It feels like they're glued to my head. But they're not. They're...growing...out of my head."

"When, um..." Dad starts, spinning his finger around like he's trying to say something without saying it. "When did you first...notice them?"

I let go of my antlers. I look at Dad through the reflection in the mirror. "Well, I kinda saw them this morning when I woke up."

Dad's eyes grow a little bigger. He didn't know!

"They were only a few inches long when I was hiding them with a hat. I didn't want you to see them because I knew you'd get mad."

"Oh, buddy," Dad says. He sounds very sorry. He reaches over and puts his arm around me, pulling me into a hug. It actually feels good. "I'm sorry. That must have terrified you."

"A little," I say. "I didn't know what else to do."

He helps me walk into the kitchen, and we sit at the counter.

"So," Dad continues, "the good news for you is I still haven't spoken to Mom yet today."

Oh, that's a relief.

"But I needed to find you some help. So...I called Gramma Dee Dee."

"Gramma?" I say surprised and a little scared.

"I did my best to describe what happened," Dad continues, "and she's coming over right now. She's offered to stay with us for as long as you need, to help you, um, de-grow your antlers. She should be here in about an hour."

"Did you tell her not to tell Mom?" I ask desperately. *Please say yes, please say yes, please say yes.*

"I told her we didn't tell Mom," Dad says. "I trust Gramma to do the smart thing."

"Are you afraid to tell Mom too?" I ask.

Dad smiles. "More than you know," he says.

Somehow, this makes me feel a whole lot better.

Rick

Dee Dee Andrews arguably reset the industry standards for

professional Muses in Hollywood, and Abby was her protégé and truly most magnificent successor. Along with setting new precedents in the artform, Dee Dee was one of the greatest scholars on the topic of the Muse Phenomenon in, quite possibly, the world. She'd written books, spoken at colleges and universities, and even worked on legislation to regulate rights and health laws for professional Muses. If I could sponsor her for an honorary PhD on the topic, I would.

Momma Dee Dee is also wonderfully eccentric. She wears vibrantly colorful clothing, thick-rimmed glasses in amazingly kooky shapes, and the brightest hues of makeup ever put to palette. When she enters a room, her presence overflows out the windows. If she wants your head on a platter, she'll tell you to your face. She's an open book, unapologetic, and most importantly, adores her family to pieces. I admire the hell out of her.

Dee Dee's sky blue station wagon pulls into our driveway, and Dee Dee herself seems to float to the front door, her long, layered skirt obstructing her confident stride and trainers. I open the door and brace for either a kiss on the cheek or a fist to the face.

She gives me one of the most amazing bear hugs I've ever endured. Momma Dee Dee is the best.

"My precious Rick," she says as she rocks me back and forth, "how are you doing, my boy?" She's in a grandmotherly mood. Thank God.

"Hanging in there, Momma," I say. "Hanging in there."

She releases me from her embrace, but not before gripping my upper arms and giving me one more shake. Even her affection is enthusiastic. Dee Dee then walks past me into the house and makes a beeline to Andy, who's been sitting in the living room quietly for the past hour, practicing his balance. It's actually been quite amusing to watch, though I don't let Andy know I've been watching.

As Dee Dee sees Andy and the impressive extensions atop his crown, she stops. Her mouth falls open and her eyes grow wide. Yep, that's what I thought when I first saw them too.

"My boy!" she exclaims, putting a hand to her chest for dramatic effect.

Andy turns around and, upon seeing his grandmother's impressive gawk, stands up and immediately stumbles to one side as the weight of his head carries him sideways. Dee Dee quickly approaches Andy and catches him before he tumbles, embracing him tightly with both arms and rocking him back and forth as she'd done to me. Andy holds tight to her as well, in part for balance and in part because he loves his grandmother.

Dee Dee soon releases her embrace and places her palms against Andy's cheeks. Andy fights not to smile. "I know this isn't what you want to hear," she says to him, "but these antlers of yours are *magnificent!*"

Andy laughs. Gramma always knows how to break her grandson.

I put myself to work in the kitchen by making dinner while I listen to Dee Dee and Andy chat in the living room. Andy tells Dee Dee about Abby's Career Day visit, the interactions with Bruno, drawing the boy with antlers, and everything that's happened today. Dee Dee listens intently and lovingly. She helps coax more detail of the last few days out of Andy. The more he shares, the more my heart breaks for him. How did I not know my son was suffering this?

Finally, Andy asks, "So, can you help me get rid of these before Mom gets home?"

Dee Dee thinks for a moment. I can't quite see from my angle, but I imagine her scrunched face and tightly pressed lips. I watch as she leans in to study the antlers carefully. "To be honest, my boy," she says, "it's difficult to say."

Andy's expression matches my internal response—fear and worry.

"You see, when a Muse grows something on their person," Dee Dee explains, "it's with a purpose. It's not just 'because.' When actors work with Creators, they don't just work on the physical form of it. They are also working on the story, the motivation behind it. That's what makes it so real. It makes it real to them. What we need to figure out is what makes your antlers real to you. Why you must have them and what you need or must do to let them go."

"How do I do that?" Andy asks nervously.

"Well, that's why I'm here!" Dee Dee says, throwing her arms in the air with great enthusiasm, as if to say, "Ta-Da!"

Andy tries not to giggle, but he can't help but release a few. Neither can I.

"The first thing to try is basic rest," she explains. "If we're lucky, the antlers will go away tonight with a good night of sleep."

Dee Dee also recommends we try to keep the evening as normal and routine as possible. I'm sure Andy hopes this means we can watch TV tonight or play video games.

"Remember, you're still grounded," I say.

Andy's face falls.

"We'll play board games tonight. How does that sound?"

Andy shrugs and nods. He's disappointed, but he understands.

Andy had many questions for Dee Dee throughout dinner and the evening. About the Muse Phenomenon. About the history and techniques used by professionals. About the physiology of transformations. Even about his grandmother's own experience. Dee Dee is all too happy to answer all his questions, and she does so at a level that even I feel I can understand. The Muse Phenomenon is a truly complex artform. The more I listen, the more I wonder and worry: how in the world did Andy do this to himself and, truly, how are we going to resolve this before his mother gets home?

When it's time to put Andy to bed, his grandmother and I contemplate a good pillow placement for him and his extensions. "Andy tends to sleep on his side," I remark.

"Well, that's hardly going to happen tonight," Dee Dee replies. "Not unless you want to cut holes in his mattress."

I raise a teasing eyebrow at Andy, garnering a look of horror.

"Don't you dare!" he threatens.

We collectively figure a mountain of pillows at his back and a more reclined posture will be his best option. Andy tests out our solutions and reluctantly agrees.

"But what if I can't even get to sleep tonight?" he asks, understandably concerned.

"Then you come find me downstairs, and I'll tell you all the stories I have about famous actors from the 1970s," Dee Dee says. "Like how I had to tag along with Diedrich Hoffer while he went to every gas station and convenience store so he could buy a single candy bar from each."

Andy blinks twice. "I don't know who that is."

Dee Dee puts a hand to her chest, her face aghast. "You don't know who Diedrich Hoffer is? My word, what are they teaching you in that pretentious school of yours?"

"Math, science, and European history," I say with a cheeky smile. "I'm afraid the lessons on classically handsome sci-fi action movie stars don't come up until middle school."

Dee Dee huffs. Andy just looks more confused. I just shrug.

"He wasn't a bad actor," I add. "Just more handsome than talented in my opinion. Though he did do a movie where he had outlandish protrusions coming out of the top of his head."

"Maybe Gramma and I could watch that together," Andy proposes expectedly.

I turn to Dee Dee. "I'm sure you might have some thoughts on that?"

Dee Dee scoffs. "Really, Richard. I was only nude for three seconds in that film."

Andy's face shifts to unmitigated horror.

"You hardly see anything. Plus, I was orange and green. Completely inoffensive."

"And with that in mind," I say, looking back at Andy, "have a good night, son."

Andy can only nod as he stares at his grandmother. I fear to think what thoughts are running through his head.

But it's probably not antlers.

* * *

I decide to take a moment to sit in the living room and just rest my...everything. I'm utterly exhausted; this day has been far too much. I collapse in my chair with an over-exasperated sigh and just close my eyes for a moment.

I had worked for nearly fifteen hours straight on these outrageous rewrites for Morgan before the call came in from Andy's school today. Upon reflection, I'm impressed I even had the strength to climb that tree to get him. I desperately want to pass out, but I still have rewrites on my mind. Seriously, how am I not growing antlers, too, by now?

Dee Dee makes us some tea and joins me in the living room. "Abby tells me you're trying again to get your miniseries made."

"Yeah," I sigh, staring down at the cup of what I assume is a form of Sleepy Time tea. "I met with Dylan Morgan yesterday and that pompous ass sent me ten pages of rewrites that he wants by tomorrow."

"That sounds about right," Dee Dee comments dismissively. "You know Reimagine Productions has been without a president for at least a month now? The board's been running the show while they determine who they want to vote in as the new head. I would bet good money Dylan is taking advantage of the moment to take all the best prospects under his control. Probably wants to build up his portfolio and put himself in position for immediate promotion. Show he can bring in the most moolah for the studio investors because he was smart enough to staple his name to already-marketable projects."

"So why did Abby set me up with him?" I ask rhetorically and a little angrily. "I thought she loved me."

"Well, if she is the one who set up the meeting, then I have a couple theories," Dee Dee says.

This piques my interest. I lean forward in my chair to listen.

"If I were to make a guess, if Dylan was to produce your story, then there's a pretty good chance he'll have his son watch it."

I raise an eyebrow at that.

"I've known that—" She wants to curse. I can see it in her eyes. "—piece of work...since he practically forced Jacqueline to marry him and have a kid. The only thing that man loves is his image. His wife has probably resigned to keeping the house in check, but look what he's doing to his son? Setting an example that the only position is the higher position. And no doubt Dylan is the dominant figure in that household. He probably treats Jacqui like...like...garbage, and then lets his boy run wild. Your story is about standing up to bullies. Maybe she wants Bruno to stand up to his dad."

"Momma," I say, "have I ever told you how infuriating you can be when you make sense?"

Dee Dee laughs, then gives me a proud wink.

"Would you mind watching Andy tomorrow while I go meet with Dylan Pompous Pants about these rewrites? It'll be in the afternoon."

"Of course!"

"Remember, he's still grounded."

"But I can still play my video games, right?"

I roll my eyes. Dee Dee laughs.

I have the best family.

Andy

I always love it when Gramma stays over. She makes the best

pancake breakfast. Dad and I love her pancakes so much. Mom can never make them quite like Gramma.

"How'd you sleep last night?" she asks me as she slides a plate of three big fluffy pancakes in front of me. She's made them just how I like them: butter, lots of syrup, and pre-cut into squares.

"I slept okay," I say. I take my fork and stack six squares onto it. The pancake squares are all dripping syrup like an overfull sponge. "It took me a little while, but then I slept until my radio went off."

"Awesome!" she says very happily. "Rest and sleep are a good start!"

Gramma squints and looks at my head. It's weird, my head feels heavier when she looks at it so closely. I feel my head dipping toward my plate, but I catch myself quickly.

"It doesn't look like we lost a lot of shape from yesterday," she says, "but that's what we're going to work on today."

"How?" I ask, my mouth full of pancakes.

"Relaxation and concentration," she says. "I'm going to teach you how to meditate."

"You're going to teach a ten-year-old with a metric ton of sugar in his system how to meditate?" I hear Dad ask as he's walking into the kitchen. He's in his pajamas and has what Mom calls "bed head." I guess he got sleep last night too.

"Hey! My magic is mine!" Gramma says, waving the spatula at Dad. I don't know what that means, but it makes Dad laugh.

"Just remember, he's still grounded," Dad says, putting a K-Cup in the Keurig. "No TV—"

"No computer, no video games. I know. I know!" Gramma says, flipping a stack of pancakes onto a plate and handing it to

Dad. "I don't suppose that list includes no music or no going outside, does it?"

Dad takes the seat next to me. I turn to look at him, and he suddenly leans back, avoiding my antlers, which, I guess, are wider than I thought.

I glance up at them. "Sorry."

"No worries, bud," he says, but he's looking weirdly at my antlers while he says it. "I'll just sit a little over here." He slides his chair about a foot away from me and sits down. I turn my head back to face Gramma. I think I see Dad flinch and lean away again.

I stuffed another bite of pancakes into my mouth. It's so weird. I can feel the antlers wobble on my head as I chew. I try to chew slowly, and the wobble slows. I chew a little faster, and my head feels like it's jiggling more.

Slow chew—wobble. Fast chew—jiggle. So weird!

I look up and realize Gramma and Dad are both staring at me. "It's my antlers," I say. "They feel weird when I chew."

Gramma looks like she's thinking really hard about what I just said. Dad just nods slowly and takes a drink of his coffee.

"Now remember," Dad says to me when he finishes his sip, "your grandmother has made a very special trip out here to help you. Be respectful of her time and listen to everything she has to say. I have some work to do this morning, and then I have a meeting in the city this afternoon. Promise you'll be good for Gramma Dee Dee?"

I nod and my head feels something between a wobble and jiggle this time. So weird!

Dad then turns to Gramma. "Dee Dee, let me know if you

need me to run any errands for you this afternoon too. You'll be staying with us again tonight, right?"

"Of course!" Gramma says, as if Dad asked a silly question. "Don't worry about me. You take care of your business. Andy's in good hands!"

"Alright," Dad says. He picks up his coffee and his plate. "I'm going to be in my office if you need me." He looks at me. "Promise you'll be good?"

I nod and wobble my antlers again. He gives me a smile before going to his office with his coffee and his pancakes.

"Gramma," I say, "what's meditation?"

"Meditation," Gramma says, putting pancakes on her plate and turning off the stove, "is clearing your mind of all distracting thoughts. You find a comfortable place to sit and just try to focus on nothing, or sometimes focus on something benign, like nature sounds or soothing music."

"And that's going to help me get rid of my antlers?" I ask.

"Well, that's my hope. If your antlers grew because you were thinking super hard about having antlers, and you had a reason for having antlers, somewhere in your mind, you still have those thoughts. We're going to try and flush all those thoughts away."

I gather all the remaining pieces of pancake into a big syrup pile on my plate. "When I poke at them, I don't feel them," I say. "Am I supposed to feel them?"

"Not normally, no," Gramma says, taking the seat next to me. "Your body would have to grow nerves into them, and you can't really grow nerves. But your brain knows they're there and makes you think you can feel your transformations, but in reality, you're not feeling them. And sometimes, depending on the circumstances, you'll still *think* you feel them, even when you don't have the transformation anymore. That feeling is what we call a 'legacy pain.'"

"Why would it hurt if it's not there anymore?" I ask. I put the last scoop of syrup and pancake crumbs in my mouth and chew slowly. Yeah, wobble feels a little better than jiggle.

"Well, it's what happens in your brain when you think about your experience with your transformation really hard," Gramma explains. "You're basically remembering the feeling. For example, I once had to transform horns out of the back of my elbows for a role where I was supposed to be a scary demon. Sometimes, when I think about that role, my elbows will tingle."

"What were you doing with horns on your elbow?" I ask. I didn't know Gramma played a demon! Cool!

"You can watch that show when you're older," she says with a smile and a wink.

Why would I have to be older before I see that? Unless...no, I don't want to think about *that* again.

* * *

Gramma and I sit on the back porch on two of Mom's couch cushions. I hope Mom won't mind that we're getting her cushions dirty. I don't need her mad at us for that too.

"Alright," Gramma says, putting her hands on her knees. "First, we're going to breathe." She takes a long breath in through her nose. She then says to hold our breath for five seconds, then to slowly breathe out for seven seconds. I think I can do that.

I take a big breath and puff out my cheeks like I do when I go swimming.

"No, no, no," she says, shaking her head. "Put the air in your chest, not your cheeks."

In my chest? I let out the breath I'm holding and take another, this time trying to keep it in my chest. I guess this is what puffing out your chest means. I hold it for five seconds. One...two...three...four...five. I then blow the air out through my mouth for seven seconds. One...two...three...four...oh no! It only took me four seconds to breathe out before I was out of air. Man, meditation is hard.

We do it all again: big breath through my nose, hold it in my chest for five seconds, blow it out of my mouth. At least I make it to five seconds this time. But now I feel like I want to yawn. Is this what meditation was supposed to feel like? If so, it's not very relaxing.

We do the breathing a bunch more times, and I can finally breathe out for seven seconds. Finally! But now I'm super yawny, and every time I yawn, my antlers wobble. I don't know if this is going to work.

Gramma pulls out her phone and a small Bluetooth speaker. Some really weird music starts playing from the speaker. It's like wind played through a keyboard or something.

"Now," Gramma says, "let's close our eyes." I close my eyes. "And we're just going to sit still, listen to the music and try not to think of anything else. Just...listen..."

I listen to the music, but I don't know what I'm supposed to be listening for. Maybe I'm supposed to figure out what the sounds are? I've never heard any of these instruments before. Is that maybe a flute? And the music doesn't really sound like it's moving. It sounds like it was just one chord played for ten seconds, then another chord for another ten seconds, then the first chord again. Then...wait. Are those frogs and birds in there too? All I can really think about is how weird this music is. Is this meditating?

I try not to think of my antlers. Or Bruno.

Or Bruno's dad.

Or Mom being mad at me.

Oh no, now I'm thinking about all those things. I think about how mad I am that Bruno called me a "Mommy's Boy." I think about how mad I am that Bruno's dad said Mom was ugly. I think about how Bruno was the one that started the fight, not me, but we both got in trouble. No, only *I* got in trouble. Why am I in trouble? He was the one who called me names and pulled at my hat. I didn't do anything to him! It's all his fault I'm in trouble! It's all his fault that—

"Listen to the music!" I hear Gramma say. She sounds mad.

I open my eyes. She's frowning at me. Did I do something wrong?

"I was listening," I say.

"Your antlers are growing," she says. Has she been watching me this whole time?

And she actually saw my antlers grow?

"You're thinking of what's making you upset," she says. "That's what we're trying *not* to think about, remember?"

I fidget a little. "Sorry."

Gramma gives me a smile. "Let's try again, shall we?"

I close my eyes again and try to listen to the music. Huh, what are these instruments making those sounds? Maybe it *is* a keyboard after all. What's that instrument called? A synthesizer or something? Maybe it's a keyboard trying to sound like a flute. It doesn't sound very good.

For some reason, the sound makes me think of the color blue. Could sounds have colors? If they do, this sound is definitely blue. Like a dark blue but with stripes of light blue. And the stripes are kinda wavy.

And the frog sound is green, because frogs are green. The birds are either red or yellow. Maybe the faster chirps are yellow and the slower chirps are red. And the red and yellow are like paint splatter on the blue wavy stripes. And the green frog sound was like a scribble.

"Very good," I hear Gramma say. "Very, very good. What you're doing now is meditating. Keep doing that."

So, listening to music and finding colors is meditating? Huh, this is actually kinda fun. Who knew mediation could be fun?

We listen to a few more songs and I try to figure out all the colors for each sound. Finally, after three or four songs, Gramma tells me I can open my eyes. She's smiling at me, like she's really proud. She tells me to get up and go to the bathroom and look in the mirror.

Oh my gosh! They've shrunk! My antlers are small again!

It's working! Maybe if I keep meditating, they'll be completely gone by the time Dad gets back from his meeting this afternoon.

And maybe we'll never have to tell Mom! Gramma is the best!

4

The Boy Who Wanted to Fight

Rick

I sit outside Dylan Morgan's office holding a printed copy of the updated manuscript. I'm making small talk with Fortune as I wait. She's finally found the fridge with the sodas and sparkling waters in the break room at the other end of the floor.

I never understood the tactic of making people wait. Perhaps it's a way of separating chaff from the wheat. Anyone weak or intimidated would quickly fly out. If Dee Dee's theories are correct, then Morgan needs me more than I need him. It matters little to me. I'm not doing this for Morgan. I'm doing this for Abby and Andy. And maybe I'm doing this for Bruno too. Well, for the Brunos of the world, I suppose. Whatever my motivation, it keeps me occupied enough to wait outside that office and chat about fridges full of soda.

I pull out my phone and look at my recent text exchanges with Abby. She's enjoying Vancouver and the progress the actors and Muses have made on this project. Apparently, her consult is for some television production about sexy teens in a supernatural town. I hate the "sexy teen" genre, but I appreciate Abby's enthusiasm for bettering the craft. I break down and tell her that Andy's been grounded for being in a fight at school, but I don't share with whom or the surrounding circumstances. I certainly don't tell her about Andy's antlers. She's disappointed but promises to keep the secret of her knowledge of his punishment until she's home on Monday. In the meantime, she sends her support and encouragement for my meeting with Morgan.

"Hey, Fortune," I say, "I was curious. Do you know if the studio has made any progress in finding a new president? I was chatting with my mother-in-law last night, and she said the studio's been without a head for a few months."

"I wouldn't know," Fortune replies bashfully. "I don't get all the news on what's going on. And Mr. Morgan doesn't talk about that stuff with me. I heard in the lunchroom, though, that they may be close to picking someone. I think they said there's an offer and they're just waiting for the person to accept. Didn't hear a name. You think it could be true? I can't tell if people are telling the truth or just starting rumors."

"Me neither," I admit. "I always hear the news from my wife and mother-in-law, and they're so deep in the industry they seem to know things before everyone else."

"Your wife is the actress, Abby Andrews, right?" Fortune asks.

"I actually rewatched *The Murder of Madam Redstone* recently. I thought she was just brilliant. She has such range."

"Oh, I will certainly let her know. She always appreciates hearing when people appreciate her acting roles."

"My sisters and I would watch *Grace Falls* around Valentine's Day, back when we were hopeless romantics. I know everyone talks about the wing scene from that movie as being the best part. It always creeped me out, personally."

"I'm with you, believe me." It was far more terrifying witnessing it live, but I don't share that.

"I'm sorry. It's probably weird to talk about your wife like that. I'm just a huge fan."

"No worries at all. I take her praises as compliments. It reminds me how amazingly lucky I am that she chose to stick with me."

Fortune giggles a bit and turns back to her computer. I return to sitting silently for another fifteen or so minutes before Morgan finally opens his office door and pokes his head out to talk to Fortune. He's holding his cell phone to his ear.

"Sweety, could you get me a grapefruit La Croix?" he asks. Before he gets confirmation, he turns to me and waves me into his office.

I turn to Fortune to thank her. She has a very confused and almost frightened expression on her face. I lean in and say to her, "The flavor is called pamplemousse." Yep, I clocked her solicitude accurately as she mouths a relieved "Thank you" to me before getting up from her desk to get his drink.

I follow Morgan into his office and sit in the guest chair he gestures to.

"Well, can you tell me as soon as you know?" he says to

whoever is on the phone, not particularly politely. "Yes, as soon as you know. Like, before you send the notice to everyone, text me first. Got it? ... Sure. Look, I have to go, I have someone in my office. ... Yeah. ... Yeah. Okay. Bye." He ends the call, places the phone face down on his desk, and sits down in his desk chair with a heavy *fump*.

Sure, as if you've been working so hard, Morgan.

"I'm so sorry," he says with such false modesty I should report him to the Actors Guild for impersonating an actor. "Gotta work on those time management skills, right?"

Isn't the top job requirement of a producer "excellent time management skills"?

"How have you been?" Morgan asks. "My son tells me he and Andy got into a fight the other day."

"Yep, Andy is grounded for a week," I say. "No TV, no computer, no video games."

"Ouch," Morgan replies with wince. "That's harsh. I mean, it was a fight between elementary school boys. How bad could it be?"

"Well, we're a zero-tolerance household when it comes to fighting and bullying," I reply, curtly. I figured he'd know that, considering the script we're working on, the pompous—

"Ah. Well, speaking of zero-tolerance...your script." Of course, that's how he's going to start the conversation. "I just finished looking through the rewrites—"

No, you didn't.

"—and, well, it's still not working."

Could you not be any more constructive in your feedback?

"Frankly I'm disappointed. You'd been working on this for years and it can't get better than this?"

I take a breath and tighten my lips. "Well, maybe if you could explain what's not working, it would help," I say rather firmly. "I went through all your notes. I changed the personas. I added the scene with the bicycle chase to add more action. I even added a 'love interest' for the boy. What's still not working?"

"Listen," Morgan starts, learning forward on his desk and folding his hands like some principal about to lecture me on responsibility. "I don't know how else to say this, but I don't think you're cut out for this. It's just not working. I mean, if you could read what I was reading, you'd see it. I can't put it into words. I just know."

That. Pompous. Ass! Oh, how I want to punch him in his stupid fake-white teeth.

"Look, you know we're going through some transitions," he continues, arrogance oozing out of him like a sponge saturated with car oil, "and our new president is going to want the best stories. This just isn't it. I don't know what else to say."

I know what *I* wanted to say...

"I know Abby pulled all kinds of strings to get your story to me," he goes on. "Do apologize to her for wasting her time. We're just not going to move forward with it."

I stand from the chair. "Well then," I say with as much composure as I can muster, "let me apologize first. Sorry for wasting your time."

"Hey, no skin off my back," Morgan says, standing from his chair. "I'll tell you what, next time you come up with an idea, send it to Fortune, and I'll read it myself."

"Thank you for the offer," I reply. "And thank you again for your time. I'll go ahead and see myself out."

"Have Fortune get you a drink on your way out!" Morgan says as I turn and leave.

If I was any other man, I would have taken that opportunity to turn around and point my finger into that jackass's face and tell him what he was full of. I would have berated him about his lack of tact and taste. And after I had punched him in his face, I would tell him my wife was the most beautiful woman in the world and he had no right to call her anything but. If I was any other man...

Instead, I walk out of his office and close the door. I don't even slam it. Fortune has just returned with a Pamplemousse La Croix. If I was any other man, I would snatch the can from her hand and take it for myself as I marched out of the office. Instead, I bow my head and thank Fortune for the small talk before I walk to the elevator.

It takes remarkable restraint not to throw my badge at Martha as I leave the building. I do regret not saying a longer goodbye to Martha on the way out. I hope she'll forgive my rudeness.

I go to my car and sit in the driver's seat. Then, finally, after great pains to hold it all in, I release my rage on my steering wheel. I scream profanities I didn't even think were in my vocabulary. I think I even start to cry.

I just know?

I just *know*?

Does he even realize how phony that line sounds? Does he really think he's so gifted in recognizing creativity and talent that he can just "know" it? He never wanted to work with me. He probably didn't even want to read my script in the first place.

There's no *way* he read all my rewrites before our meeting. He just wanted to waste my time and blame Abby for all of it.

He's always been jealous of Abby. He's always been jealous of us. Her movie saved the studio, not his. Her movies grossed better than his. He was always a second-rate actor, a tenth-rate producer, and a millionth-rate father. He only kept his producer position because he didn't jump ship when the past president stepped down. He probably thinks he could single-handedly save the studio with what he "knows." What an ignorant, moronic, asinine, imbecilic, brainless, pompous *ass*!

I freeze. I catch myself reaching for my head and feeling my crown.

No. I'm not growing antlers.

I think I just need to go home and be with my son. My anger and frustration can wait. What's truly important is that he's recovering. Yes, I just need to be home with my family. That'll calm me.

I wonder, if I asked, if Momma Dee Dee would make pancakes for dinner tonight. I could really go for Dee Dee's pancakes.

Andy

Gramma slams her laptop closed right as we hear the front door open. She was playing her video games, and I "wasn't" watching.

I hear Dad throw his keys onto the side table by the door. It sounds like he threw them really hard. Oh no, is he upset? Did his meeting go really badly?

Dad comes around the corner through the kitchen and sees Gramma standing behind the couch, not playing on her laptop.

I stand up, too, and look at Dad. He looks mad...but not at me. Something about how he looks actually makes me sad.

Then Dad looks at me and starts to look less mad. It almost looks like he's going to cry.

"Look at you," he says, his voice cracking. Wow, he sounds like he's going to cry too. "You're looking so much better." He walks around the couch and hugs me tight. "I'm so glad. So glad you're getting better."

"Gramma helped a lot," I say.

Dad pulls back and holds my shoulder tight. He's definitely crying, but he's also smiling. I don't think I've ever seen Dad cry before.

"How did your meeting go today?" I ask.

Dad looks down and squeezes my shoulders a little bit. "Not great," he says, "but that's okay. What's important is that your day went well, right?"

"Sure." I'm not sure what that means exactly, but I smile.

"Sweety," Gramma says very gently, "could you give your father and I a moment? Why don't you go ahead and put your sketchbook back upstairs and maybe try and take a nice hot shower."

"Okay," I say.

Dad lets go of my shoulders and I head upstairs. Gramma and Dad watch me leave. That only happens when Mom and Dad don't want me to hear what they're going to talk about.

I wonder how bad Dad's meeting really went.

Rick

"...and then he said 'I just know.' I just *know*? What does he think he sounds like?" I can't contain my anger, and I'm beyond grateful that Dee Dee was astute enough to send Andy away so I could vent. "So, I'm just going to be done. No more meeting with Dylan 'Pompous Ass' Morgan anymore. I'll explain it all to Abby when she gets home, and we'll just move on. I'm done."

"Good for you," Dee Dee says in support.

"Yeah, well..." My words trail off as I notice I've been pacing the living room the entire time. I haven't even sat down since I got home. I collapse in my reading chair and take a deep breath. "Well, it's going to be a little while before I want to deal with that script again," I admit. "Y'know? It's funny. While I was sitting in my car, just screaming and feeling myself getting so angry, I actually got worried that *I* was starting to grow antlers. I guess I understand just that much more what Andy's going through. How was his day?"

"Well, you saw his progress," Dee Dee replies proudly. "We did some meditating, and he figured out how to shift his concentration. We'll see how he is tomorrow morning, but I think with a little more time we can get everything down and gone."

"That is the best news I've heard today," I say with immense relief. "I was thinking I'd take him to school tomorrow to get his books and things, and we'll just take it easy through the weekend. Give us room to breathe and start fresh on Monday when Abby gets back."

"Phenomenal idea, Rick!" Dee Dee exclaims, with her trademark loving enthusiasm.

I'm truly starting to feel better. Maybe I'll take a day or two to recalibrate, perhaps read a book, maybe start one of my other projects. The idea of taking a few days off with Andy is remarkably refreshing. I even start to think, maybe, when Abby gets home, we can plan a family vacation. Get away from our life here for a week or two. Wouldn't that be just the best?

I let out another trapped breath and hop up from my chair, feeling somewhat renewed. "Since I assume you're going to hang around another night," I say to my mother-in-law, "could I possibly trouble you to make pancakes for dinner?"

"For you boys," Dee Dee says, "of course!"

"Yes!" Andy exclaims from the stairs, having finished his shower and dressed for bed. "Can we watch TV too?"

"You're still grounded," I say.

Andy pouts. "Awww, c'mon!"

He'll get over it. His half-smile gives him away.

Andy

My antlers are even smaller! I woke up this morning, and when I sat up, no wobble or jiggle. I run to the bathroom and look in the mirror. They are so small they're practically hidden under my hair! This is great! This means I can easily hide them under a hat today without even worrying if anyone thinks I have something stuck to my head.

Dad takes me to school so we can get my books and a list of the work I missed so I can work on it over the weekend. When we arrive at my school, we stopped at Mr. Foldger's office so Dad can talk about his "deep concern" about how the school didn't do much to help me when I was being bullied or when I ran away. Mr. Foldger just keeps nodding and agreeing with Dad and promises to do better in the future. It's weird that he didn't really apologize.

Mr. Foldger then takes us down the hall to my locker to get my things. Dad says that's all we have to do, and then we can go home.

I take out my bag and all my books, as well as my lunch bag which, well, I'm afraid to look in. I wonder what happens to a turkey sandwich when it's stuck in a locker for three days.

Dad takes a quick look inside my bag. "Didn't you have another sketchbook you brought to school?"

"It's probably in my desk," I say. "I don't need it. We can go."

"Your other one's almost full," Dad says. "Why don't you go and grab it quickly?"

Aww, man. I don't really want to go into my classroom. But I don't want to make Dad mad. "Fine. One sec."

I turn to my classroom door and reach for the knob. I peek in through the window, and...

Oh no! I totally forgot! Bruno's dad is here for Career Day.

"What's wrong?" Dad asks.

"Um, Bruno's dad is here," I say. "I don't wanna go in."

Dad doesn't say anything right away, which is weird. Usually, Dad would try to get me to go anyway. Instead, he turns to Mr. Foldger.

"Would you mind getting his sketchbook for him?" he asks my principal. "It's the one with the dark green cover, right, Andy?"

I nod. Mr. Foldger nods and goes into the classroom for me. I try to stand out of the way of the door where no one can see us. Dad does the same. He looks kinda nervous and maybe a little mad. He's pressing his lips together really tightly.

Through the open door, we can hear Mr. Morgan talking to the class. "Oh, all the time! I meet a lot of famous people," we hear him say. He's probably answering questions. "Mostly we talk about movies. Sometimes even on the movie set. And they all love to talk to me. It's like we're all friends."

Dad leans over and whispers to me really quietly, "That's not true. Bruno's dad works on cartoons and animation projects now. He doesn't go to movie sets anymore."

Bruno's dad is a liar? I'm so going to tease Bruno about that when I get back to school on Monday.

Someone then asks a question that I can't quite hear. Mr. Morgan answers, "I'm working on a lot of things right now actually. Let's see...Oh! One of the newest things I'm working on is a project I actually wrote myself. You want to know what it's called?"

The class sounds a little excited to hear, but not very.

"It's called *The Boy Who Grew Antlers*."

Wait...what? Did he just say he wrote a project called *The Boy Who Grew Antlers*?

I can feel Dad grasp my shoulder really hard, right as Mr. Morgan says that. I look up. Dad is super, super angry. He's staring at the door like he wants to tear it off the wall and throw it.

Then, I remember Dad's meeting yesterday. Wasn't it about his script? The one called *The Boy Who Grew Antlers*? Was he meeting with...Bruno's dad?

Before I know what I'm doing, I run into the classroom. I barely hear Dad trying to call me back.

"Liar!" I scream at Mr. Morgan. "You didn't write that story!" I see Bruno standing next to Mr. Morgan. He looks shocked.

"Andy, what are you doing?" Mr. Foldger says. He's annoyed with me, but I'm too angry to care.

"You didn't write that!" I scream again. "That's my dad's story! Not yours! You're a liar!"

"Andy, Andy, Andy," Mr. Morgan says with a really creepy smile. "Your dad gave me his story. He said I could write it." Mr. Morgan looks past me, and his creepy smile turns into a shocked look.

I turn around and see Dad standing in the doorway.

"Hey, Dylan," Dad says, looking like he still wants to tear off the door. "I said you could do what now?"

Everyone in the room is quiet. Mr. Morgan looks like he's trying to smile, but he can't. Bruno looks super embarrassed. Everyone else is just looking at us.

"You stole my dad's story!" I yell at him again. I step forward and...

On no! My head's wobbly again. *No...please no...*

I look around. Everyone is getting up from their desks and slowly moving toward the edges of the room, away from me.

"Andy," I hear Dad say. He sounds a little scared. "Don't move too quickly, bud."

I can't help it. I reach up and feel my head. It's what I was afraid of. My antlers grew back! Not only did they grow back, they grew big!

I stretch my arms all the way up, and I still can't reach the top. Oh no...

I try to turn around to face Dad. I hear some of the kids in the class scream. My antlers are so heavy and wobbly, my head falls forward, and my antlers crash into the desk. It hurts so bad it feels like my hair's being ripped out of my head.

I lift my head back up. It's super heavy and super wobbly, but I manage to stand up straight. I turn my head a little, and my whole body turns around. More people scream as I knock into desks and chairs. I'm facing Mr. Morgan again. He looks scared and angry.

But I'm more angry.

I'm more angry at Mr. Morgan than anyone else in the whole world. Even more than Bruno.

I want to ram Mr. Morgan so badly I can feel it in my whole body.

He's the one who called Mom ugly.

He's the one who made Dad upset.

He's the one who didn't stop Bruno from bullying me.

"It's your fault!" I scream at him, as I feel my antlers growing even bigger. "It's all your fault!!"

Rick

I hand my phone to Mrs. Perkins as she and Mr. Foldger finish filing all the kids out of the classroom. "Go into the contacts and call Dee Dee Andrews," I instruct her. "That's Andy's grandmother. She's been helping him out. Tell her to get here right away."

Mrs. Perkins nods and hurries out of the room.

Morgan and Bruno are still standing at the front of the room. Morgan is clearly freaking out, but the idiot is still trying to act stoic. Even annoyed. What an idiot. Bruno looks scared to death.

"How dare you accuse me!" Morgan exclaims at my son. "I did nothing to you. You're the one threatening me!"

"Shut up!" Andy cries. He's furious and probably terrified. "You called my mom ugly! You stole my dad's story! You're a jerk! I hate you! This is all your fault!"

"Bennett, put your boy in his place," Morgan demands, his fear breaking through his facade.

Carefully, I take a few more steps into the classroom. I'm not sure Andy can tell, but his antlers...they're gigantic! They've nearly reached the ceiling in height, and it appears, at the rate they're expanding, they very soon will. If he's not careful, they'll swallow the room!

I take another step closer. "Andy?" I say gently and calmly.

Possibly out of instinct, Andy whips his head around, his massive antlers swinging his whole body with him. I've clearly misjudged the reach of his antlers, because right as he turns, one of his antlers hits me square in the eye. I grab my eye and stagger back as if I've been punched. That's going to sting in the morning.

"Dad!" Andy calls out, frightened.

Oh, my poor boy. I know he didn't mean to hit me.

Just then, Morgan lets out a loud burst of laughter at my expense.

Smart move, jackass!

As I figured he would, Andy whips his head back around. I don't get the clearest look, as I'm still clutching my own injury, but somehow Morgan must have gotten into the antlers' path of fire, because the next thing I see is him staggering backward and grabbing at his mouth. Andy must have hit him in the lip! If I was any other kind of man, I would have laughed at his pain at that moment.

"Damn kid," Morgan curses, clutching his chin. "You hit me in the face! How dare you hit me in the face?"

Andy tries to turn around again, but his antlers suddenly catch in the drop-ceiling tiles. Three foam tiles crashed to the floor, and one of the lights in the ceiling suddenly cuts out. Andy shakes his head, but he can't break free. He screams in frustration and starts to cry.

"Andy," I say. "It's going to be alright."

"Shut your kid up, Bennett!" Morgan orders. "Shut him up!"

I'm completely overwhelmed. My right eye is in extreme pain, I need to get to my son, who is terrified beyond measure, and a man I loathe with every fiber of my being is being condescending to me from the other side of the room.

And all this time, poor Bruno is huddled in a far corner, probably scared out of his mind. What a sight. God, I wish—

Just then, there's a soft knock at the door. A voice from the other side calls through, "I'm coming in."

I know that voice.

And it isn't Dee Dee's.

5

The Boy Who Got in Trouble

Rick

I turn to face the doorway. Like a beacon of hope, a savior, an angel, she walks in. I don't know whether to laugh or to cry...because I'm sure when this is all over, she'll kill me.

"Thank you, Mrs. Perkins," she says before entering the classroom and gently shutting the door. She first looks at Andy, her expression sad, disappointed, but very much full of concern.

"Mom?" Andy says through tears and snot.

"Sweetheart," Abby says gingerly, "I'm going to help Bruno and his dad get out of the room, okay? I'm going to need you to sit still for a minute. Can you do that?"

Somehow Andy nods, though it's more of a bob of his chin. His mother smiles warmly.

Abby looks about the room and zeros in on a poster within Andy's line of sight. "Can you focus on that frog poster for a few minutes? Just look at the poster, okay? You don't need to do anything else."

"Okay," Andy says with a choke and a hiccup. He obediently turns his eyes to the poster and focuses. Such a good boy.

Abby then turns to me. I'm still holding my injured eye. "Are you alright?" she asks sincerely. I nod. "He got you with an antler?"

"Nothing I didn't deserve, I suppose," I say, hoping the levity will lighten the air. My beloved gives me a sympathetic and loving smile. Good, she still loves me.

Abby then slowly makes her way across the room to where Bruno is huddled. I watch as Dylan follows her steps. He's growing more and more flustered, as if he's jealous that Abby chose his son over him. Abby never takes her gaze off Bruno.

"Don't you touch him!" Dylan demands as Abby kneels down in front of Bruno.

Her head whips in Dylan's direction, her eyes staring daggers at the sorry excuse for a father. "Your son is scared out of his mind!" Abby bites back. "Do him a favor and shut up for one second so we can get him to safety."

Dylan says nothing. She's squarely put the pompous ass in his place. Still, Abby keeps her eyes on Dylan for an extra three or four seconds. If looks could kill, Dylan would have been dead ten times before he hit the ground. God, I love this woman.

Abby then turns back to Bruno, who is now crying and shaking against the back wall. "Are you okay, buddy?" Abby asks in the most gentle and sincere voice. "Did you get hurt?"

Bruno shakes his head. He's looking Abby right in the eyes. Good for him.

"I'd like to help you out," Abby says, reaching a hand to Bruno. "Will you take my hand and let me help you?"

Bruno glances up at his dad out of instinct, as if to ask his dad's permission. His dad gives him no message that I can tell. Dylan's stunned silent. Pathetic.

Bruno turns back to Abby and reaches his hand out. Abby takes it firmly and helps Bruno to his feet. She then guides him to the door, carefully maneuvering him around the fallen chairs and splayed desks. They reach the classroom door, and she lets him out. Once he's out, she shuts the door again.

Abby then turns and says to Dylan, "You're safe to leave if you want." There is no gentleness in her voice. It almost sounds like she's challenging him.

Dylan continues to hold his mouth as he takes three hesitant side steps, taking care to clear the range of the antlers. He then walks toward the door but first stops to face Abby.

"You'll be hearing from my lawyer, you know," he threatens, pointing his finger in Abby's face. "And you'll be paying my medical bills."

"You have a busted lip at most," Abby scoffs. "If you want me to pay for your ice pack, send me the bill, you baby. Right now, pretend like you're a decent father and go make sure your son is alright, you pompous ass."

I've never felt more attracted to my wife in my entire life. Dylan, without words of rebuttal in his minuscule brain, quickly exits the classroom shutting the door behind him. Abby turns to me again and smiles, possibly amused at the stupid grin on my face. She gives me a loving nod, then goes to save our son.

Andy

I feel like I've been staring at that frog poster for hours. My head is pounding, and I can't move, well, at all. I've never been more scared and confused and angry in my whole life.

I can't hear what Mom says to Bruno or Mr. Morgan. I think I hear something about a "pompom sass," whatever that is. I turn my eyes as much as I can toward the door to see who walks in or out. Then I see Mom walking toward me. She moves the desks that were next to me out of the way and takes one of the chairs and puts it in front of me. She then sits down and scoots as close as she can to me. When she sits down, I'm taller than her again. I'm so scared she's mad at me, I start to cry again, but Mom takes my cheeks in her hands and wipes my tears with her thumbs like she used to do when I was little.

"Can I examine your head for a second?" she asks me quietly. "I just want to see how hurt you are, okay?"

"Okay," I say with a sniff.

She stands up just a little and leans over me to look at the top of my head. I feel her fingers touch around the bottom of the antlers where they're connected to my head. It stings a little, like skin being pulled tight. I wince and cry a little.

"I'm sorry, sweetie," she says quietly.

"It's okay."

Mom sits back down again and puts her hands on my cheeks. She's smiling at me. Like she's not mad.

"Are you...mad at me?" I ask. I'm about to cry a lot. I can feel it. "I'm sorry I grew antlers and broke the classroom. I didn't mean to—"

"Shhh," she says, wiping more tears from my face. "It's okay.

Gramma told me everything that happened. With you and Bruno and about your antlers. That's why I came home early."

Oh man. Gramma tattled on me. It's weird I'm not mad about that, though.

"She said you and Bruno had a nasty fight at school and that's why you grew antlers. I bet that's been super scary."

"Yeah," I say, still crying.

"And Bruno was calling you names, like Momma's Boy, huh?"

"Uh huh."

"Are you upset with me for talking to Bruno in class that day?"

I take a big sniff. "Uh uh."

Mom's smile grows a little bigger. "Do you know how *The Boy Who Grew Antlers* ends?"

"No," I say, sniffling some more.

"In the story," Mom says, "the boy confronts his bully in the park by the lake. The boy is sooo angry with his bully that he wants to ram him with his antlers and show his bully that he was the stronger one of the both of them.

"But before he does, the boy notices that the bully is cowering against a tree. His bully is really scared, more scared than the bully ever made the boy. The boy realizes he doesn't really mean to scare his bully. He only wished to prove he was stronger. He thought proving he was stronger would make him stop bothering him.

"The boy then catches a glimpse of himself in the lake and sees just how scary he looked with a huge rack of antlers on his head. The boy, too, gets scared of what he looks like, and after that, the antlers disappear. The boy apologizes to his bully for scaring him and then goes home." Mom pauses for a second and wipes more tears off my cheeks. "Kind of a lame ending, isn't it?" she says.

I laugh and Mom smiles.

Oh no. I wonder if Dad heard me laugh.

"Do you understand the lesson of the story?" Mom asks.

"I think," I say, "that the real lesson is that the boy didn't need to be stronger or better than his bully. Because if you try to be stronger or better, you can actually become someone meaner or scarier."

Mom nods.

I continue. "When the boy saw what he looked like, he was scared of himself. And he didn't want to be scary or mean like the bully."

"He wanted to be the bigger man, as they say," Mom says. "And you know what you don't need to be the bigger man?"

"What?" I ask.

Mom runs her thumbs over the top of my head again. "Antlers."

I reach up and touch my head. I can't believe it! The antlers are gone!

My head still hurts a little bit, but the antlers are completely gone! Not even nubs! Oh my gosh, I'm so happy I start crying again. I give Mom a big hug and cry on her shoulder. She hugs me back tightly. Then I feel Dad wrap his arms around the both of us. I can't believe it! I feel so much better. And I'm very, very happy.

Rick

The school called an ambulance, as well as the families of all the kids in Andy's class. Gramma Dee Dee is also waiting for us outside. Apparently, Abby had just arrived at the house from the airport when Mrs. Perkins called Dee Dee to let her know about the incident with Andy. Coincidence truly is a godsend.

Andy and I sit outside the ambulance with our respective ice packs, one for my eye and one for the top of Andy's head. The first responder and Dee Dee had examined Andy's head where the antlers had grown and determined he would probably have some bad bruising for a few days and a couple small bald spots for a little while, but he was otherwise fine. I, on the other hand, will have a black eye for a few days, but otherwise no long-term damage. Just short-term street cred, I suppose.

Dylan stands off to the side on his phone, holding an ice pack on his lip, occasionally pulling it away to look at it, as if expecting to see blood gushing from the injury. Abby called it right. He has a fat lip and nothing else. Jacqueline, Bruno's mother, arrived after all the calls to the family were made. She's with Bruno, who appears to be doing much better. Dylan's primary focus is on his lip and his phone.

Abby tours the classroom with Mr. Foldger and Mrs. Perkins to take pictures and assess all the damages. She then takes the time to greet and speak with all the parents of the kids from Andy's class, who are all gathered on the sports field outside the building for safety. I observe from my perch on the back of the ambulance as she checks on every single child and talks to every family individually. Once she's finished making her rounds, she makes her approach toward the Morgans. Before she does, I watch her pull out her phone to make a phone call. She waves for me to join her. I excuse myself from Andy and Dee Dee and join Abby on the field.

"Yeah, I'm about to talk to him now," I hear her say on the phone as I approach.

"What's going on?" I ask.

"I figured you'd want to witness this," she says with a sly smile. She takes my hand and pulls me along with her to meet with the Morgans. Of course, Abby first approaches Bruno and Jacqueline to make sure everything is still alright and that Bruno is unharmed. Bruno seems to hide behind his mother as they speak. Jacqueline, to my surprise and to her credit, is extremely gracious and thankful for Abby's concern. Everyone goes silent when Dylan approaches.

"That was my lawyer," Dylan snaps as he slides his phone into his pocket. "We're going to be suing you for damages. We're going to take everything from you, and we're going to make sure they take Andy away from you too."

The words stab me in the gut. How dare this man threaten to take away our son! And what kind of example is this setting for his own son? Outrageous!

I look at Abby to gauge her reaction. She appears completely unfazed. In fact, she appears rather confident.

"Is it true that you were going to steal my husband's script and claim it as your own?" Abby asks very matter-of-factly.

Jacqueline gasps and turns to Dylan in shock.

Dylan stammers, "I...well...you can't prove that."

"Well, I asked all the kids in our sons' class, and they said you claimed to have created a story called *The Boy Who Grew Antlers*," Abby counters. "Mrs. Perkins and Mr. Foldger heard the same as well."

"But...But..." Dylan starts, still stammering through his words, "I didn't say I was stealing it from Rick or anything."

"Do you know how long my husband has been working on this story?" Abby continues on. "About eleven years. He started it when we were pregnant with Andy. And do you know who he consulted with as he was writing it?"

Dylan freezes. He's completely petrified. I can feel a sinfully satisfying smile grow on my face. I'd nearly forgotten whom I had consulted. And now I know who Abby called and still has on the phone.

Abby picks up her cell phone again and holds it in front of her. Dylan turns ghostly white as he registers the contact name displayed on the phone's screen. "Walter," she says loudly, assuring her voice can be heard by everyone around and also through the speaker on the phone, "I'm here with Dylan Morgan. Dylan, I figured you'd be interested in speaking with the new president of Reimagine Productions, Walter Saint James."

Whatever color that remained on Dylan's face drains. He's so devoid of color, he's practically transparent now.

"Yes, I accepted the offer yesterday afternoon," Walter says over the phone. "We sent out the announcement to the studio this morning. I guess you missed it while you were at your son's Career Day talk."

"M...M...Mr. Saint James." Dylan can barely make the words.

I can barely contain my sheer unapologetic joy at watching Dylan's ego collapse right in front of us. Abby was correct. I did, indeed, work with Walter on the impetus of the story. In fact, it was Walter's idea that the boy grow deer antlers, as opposed to elk or moose. He thought the organic shape of deer antlers was more interesting and a better representation of growth and maturity over time.

"I made an appointment with your lovely assistant, Fortune, to meet with you Monday morning," Walter continues. "I trust you'll be there."

"Yes...Yes, sir," Dylan replies.

"Good!" Walter says. "Oh! Abby, is Rick there with you?"

"He's right next to me, Walter," she says proudly.

"Rick, my boy!" Walter says. "How have you been?"

"I'm well, sir," I answer. "Congratulations on the new position. We should all get together and celebrate."

"That sounds lovely," Walter replies. "We'll figure out the details later. I just wanted to say hello. Abby, glad you made it home safe. And hope young Andrew is faring well. We'll catch up soon."

"You got it, Walter," Abby says with a satisfied smile. "Take care." She ends the call and looks back at Dylan, who is barely able to make eye contact with even the grass. "So, we'll be hearing from your lawyer?" she asks with a knowing smile.

"No, you won't," Jacqueline interjects. "Thank you so much again for getting Bruno out safely. Tell Andy we hope he feels better soon."

"Thank you, Jacqui," Abby replies sincerely. "Call me if you need anything."

Jacqueline grabs Dylan's arm and escorts him and Bruno off the field.

I look at Abby with great astonishment and immeasurable pride. "How...How...?"

"Walter texted me yesterday to let me know he accepted the job," she explains. "I told him he should reach out to Dylan and see about the progress on your story. I had no idea Dylan was going to try and claim it for himself. It must be better than I'd thought."

I laugh. I can't help it. "I don't deserve you," I say.

"Probably not," she responds, "but I'm keeping you anyway."

She takes my arm and together we walk back to the ambulance, where Andy and Dee Dee have been watching the whole exchange. Andy's expression truly encapsulates the moment: pure and unfiltered shock and amazement. Abby pulls Andy in for a big hug.

"So, how bad's the damage?" Dee Dee asks.

"Well," Abby starts, letting Andy go, but keeping one arm around him, "it doesn't look like there's too much to fix in the classroom except a few tiles and the light fixture. I offered to pay for damages, but Mr. Foldger refused. He said it was the least they could do for not doing more to help Andy. Plus, the school's insurance should cover most everything. I talked with all the kids and their parents. No one got hurt, but we'll probably have to throw an apology dinner party or something for everyone. The only one who threatened legal action was Dylan, but Jacqui will put a stop to that." Abby then looks at Andy and me with a very stern and serious scowl. "Now, for you two."

Here we go...

"You're both grounded!"

"What?!" Andy and I say in unison and equal shock.

"For you," Abby says to Andy, "no TV, no computer, no video games for a week."

"But—" Andy starts before his mother cuts him off.

"And as for you," she says, looking me straight in the eyes, "no writing for a month."

"But—" I catch myself and pause for a quick second. "Y'know what? I think I can manage that." I look over at Andy.

Our son smiles. "Yeah," he says. "I think I can too."

Two

The Girl Who Grew Wings

1

The Boy Who Met an Angel

"I'm not going to let you go!"

The torrential rainfall masked the tears streaming down Grant's face as he confessed his love to Celeste. Celeste looked up at Grant with a great pain in her eyes.

"No!" she cried out, her own tears flooding her cheeks. "You don't know what you're asking to be with me. You don't know...what I am!"

Grant stepped forward taking Celeste's face in his hands, bringing her closer to his. "It doesn't matter to me. Because I love you." Grant leaned in to give Celeste a kiss.

Their lips barely touched when Celeste suddenly stepped back and keeled over. She shrieked in pain and fell to her hands and knees. Grant knelt down and reached to grab her.

"Stay back!" Celeste screamed, her body shaking.

Just then, Grant noticed a movement coming from Celeste's

back, under her blouse. Grant backed away as the movements grew more violent. Celeste cried in pain. Grant stepped back and watched in horror. Two forms tore through the back of her blouse. From her back, the forms began to stretch and grow out, like horns or spikes.

Or *wings*. Celeste...was growing wings.

Grant kept a safe but close distance as the growths continued to stretch out from Celeste's back. Each wing was now three feet long. Five feet. Eight feet. From the stretched skin, fine silky white hairs also grew. Like gentle feathers. Celeste's painful cries were visceral. They tore into Grant's core. He brought his hands to his mouth, covering his shock and suppressing his terror. Celeste let out one last painful scream as her wings finished developing into their final majestic form. She gasped in pain. All she could do was breathe heavily. Breathe and weep with pain.

Grant tried to take a step forward but was stopped when Celeste put a hand up.

"Stay back!" she screamed through anguished tears. Celeste lifted one leg to get her footing. She pushed herself up, struggled to get her balance, but still managed to stand, despite the weight of her newly formed and amazing wings. Her torn blouse barely covered her torso as she looked back at Grant.

"It's true," Grant said, now crying himself. "You're...an angel."

Rick

"And *cut!*"

Everyone on set erupts in applause as the rain machines are shut off. The set lights are brought to full illumination. There isn't a dry eye in the house, and not because of the fake downpour. Abby's expression turns to relief as Mason, her costar, applauds her performance, also with tears in his eyes. He's probably the only one in the room that could possibly imagine what Abby's endured. He's clearly very proud of her, as am I.

Also, he's clearly worried for her. As am I.

"That was amazing," he exclaims as he reaches out to give Abby a strong hug.

Abby grabs onto Mason, both to return the hug and for extra stability.

"Alright, everyone," the medic on set calls out, "get Abby a stool. Careful grabbing her wings! Don't push too hard. You'll strain her back!"

Meredith, Abby's assistant on set, brings the stool and sets it just behind her as Mason, still acting as her stabilizer, assists her onto the seat.

I sit on the sideline with Walter. While everyone applauds, I have one hand gripping my knee and the other squeezing Walter's hand. While everyone else is overjoyed with the success of her live transformation, I am terrified. Terrified and angry. She's clearly put herself through so much pain—she's clearly in so much pain now—and there's nothing I can do.

Walter frees his hand from my grip and puts it on my shoulder. He looks at me with care and tears in his eyes. "Go on," he says to me with a warm smile. "She's probably most anxious to see you anyway."

I get up from my seat and force my way through the sea of people to get to Abby. Mason must have seen my efforts, as he assists in making a path for me. A medic is checking Abby's condition, as several PAs with towels are drying her hair and "wings" off. A few crew place rigs under the wings to help support them and remove the strain on Abby's back, as well as keep them off the wet ground, as other PAs with hair dryers work to dry everything off.

After the medic finishes speaking to Abby, Mason pushes me forward to take his place before anyone else can get in the way. I fall to my knees and take both her hands in my left hand, and her face in my right. I give her approximately a thousand kisses. Abby giggles in between them all and takes my face in her hands.

"How was I?" she asks with a smile. She is still very much crying from, I can only assume, everything.

"Magical," I reply through my own smile and tears. "Are you okay? Are you in pain?"

"I'll be alright," she says half-heartedly.

A voice from a loudspeaker announces a ten-minute cleanup before Abby is needed for her photo shoot. The production needs to take full advantage of Abby's wings for continuity in both the film and promotional photography, and since no Muse has ever created anything so large, let alone had the transformation choreographed and filmed, they want to get as much content as possible out of the opportunity. Understandable. Cruel, but understandable. After all, Hollywood is a business, and time is money.

Walter, along with the medical professionals, estimate Abby can sustain her wings for no more than six hours, and she is going to need them, not only for the photographs, but at least one other scene in the movie.

"Talk to me about our wedding," Abby says after the announcement. "Where are we on the planning?"

"Okay," I start. "Well, we have the cake tasting planned a week from Saturday. The florist sent photos of arrangements she thinks you might like. My mom and sister are still waiting for your approval on their dresses. My dad wants me to go with him to his suit fitting next week. What else? Walter is still looking forward to walking you down the aisle and can't stop talking about it, and Dee Dee is looking forward to meeting my parents. Oh! I have to remember to check with Mason, to see if he wants to bring a plus one so we have the final guest count. Um...what am I missing?"

"That sounds amazing," Abby replies lovingly. "You're a wonderful wedding planner. I'm still sorry I can't do more right now."

I give Abby another kiss. "You don't need to do anything but show up," I say, squeezing her hands gently. "You could show up to the church in sweatpants for all I care, as long as we get to leave married to each other." This makes Abby laugh and blush. I love when I can make her blush.

"Five minutes!"

The PAs hurry to finish drying Abby off as the medics inject a painkiller into Abby's back at the base of each wing. Walter joins us. He gives her a kiss on the temple. I like Walter. I like him because he loves Abby.

"You were marvelous," Walter says, like only a proud teacher and mentor would. He then adds, "I promise I will never let this happen to you again. That was too much. I'm so sorry."

"Oh, no! Don't worry!" Abby replies. "I'm fine. This is fine. And it will be over soon. Thank you for all your help. I wouldn't have been able to do this without your help. Did everything come out as you envisioned?"

"Better than I envisioned," Walter says.

Abby's assistant approaches and explains she needed to get Abby to the next building over for her photoshoot. It's a covert affair, as production wants to keep the reveal a secret until the film's release. Walter and I each take one of Abby's arms and help her to her feet. A couple other assistants gently take her wings, and we all slowly, carefully, walk her out of the soundstage to a special set for the photo shoot. Walter and I pass her on to the photographer's assistants. We stay back and watch as they set up lighting and position her for photos. Mason joins shortly after they get started. He will need to be photographed with Abby too. His hair is dry, and his makeup has been reapplied. He looks good.

"How are you holding up?" he asks me.

"To be honest," I say, "I never want to see her do that ever again."

"Me neither," Mason replies genuinely. "You make sure to protect her, alright? I'm counting on you."

"Oh, before I forget," I say. "Are you bringing a plus one?"

"Yes!" Mason exclaimed. "I'm so sorry. My RSVP never got in the mail, but I am. His name's Thomas."

* * *

The twentieth anniversary of the release of the award-winning feature film, Grace Falls *is creating a real buzz in Hollywood as Reimagine Productions plans to release the remastered film for a limited showing this November. The dark romance about a fallen angel, who finds herself in a small mountain town in Colorado and falls in love with the local preacher's son, gripped the hearts of audiences worldwide.*

The most memorable and often-cited scene from the film—

that of the fallen angel, Celeste, revealing her angel wings to love interest, Grant—both gripped and frightened audiences when it was first seen in movie theaters. The revolutionary scene, performed by actress and legendary Muse, Abby Andrews, created controversy after the film's release, as it not only depicted a live example of the Muse Phenomenon, but the actress also produced the largest bodily transformation of any Muse in any movie role at the time or since. Muse unions, as well as medical professionals, protested the scene as irresponsible to the safety of Muses. Andrews did not perform as a Muse in movies for five years after the release of the film. Her last credited role as a Muse was in the sci-fi feature film Sun Spot: Solar Core, *the sequel to the sci-fi epic* Sun Spot *where Andrews reprised her role as High Priestess Gillian Arestra. Andrews continued acting regularly until the birth of her son with husband, screenwriter and children's author, Rick Bennett.*

I've always found it strange to see my name written in a periodical. At least they spelled it correctly. Two n's, two t's.

Abby's schedule is jam-packed with press dates, interviews, and personal appearances in preparation for the twentieth anniversary of the release of *Grace Falls*. The studio warned us six months ago that they were going to be releasing the remaster to celebrate the anniversary, but we were not prepared for the unimaginable schedule. We were, however, partially prepared for Tracy Reynolds, Abby's personal assistant, to be out on maternity leave a month before the release. But here we are, wrangling Abby's schedule, planning her travels, interviews, and television appearances.

And by "we," I literally mean Abby and myself. When we learned of Tracy's pregnancy, I stepped in to be Abby's assistant's assistant, to prepare to take the torch when Tracy did have to take her leave of absence. I set aside my creative writing for email writing and taking dictation. I've actually found myself enjoying the challenge. It's a change of pace for my brain, plus it gives me the opportunity to spend more time with my amazing wife and watch her dominate meetings and catch interviewers off guard with her quick wit. God, I love this woman.

I take a sip of my coffee and continue to scroll through the article on my tablet. Andy trudges down the stairs, dragging his book bag behind him.

"Hey!" Abby calls out to him from the kitchen. "What did I tell you about dragging your backpack like that?"

"That you wouldn't replace it if it tore," Andy replies, picking it up and throwing it over his shoulder begrudgingly. He opens the fridge and pulls out the milk. He opens the carton to drink from the spout, but Abby snatches it from his hand and pours milk into a glass she's already holding.

"And what did I tell you about drinking from the carton?" she says sternly.

"That if I wanted to, I should buy my own milk," he replies with a subtle sulk. Andy should know by now he isn't going to escape his mother's keen observation skills. "Why do you keep doing that?"

"Doing what?" Abby asks, handing him the glass of milk she's just poured for him. "Being your mother? It's my number one priority."

Andy pulls out the stool next to me and plops himself down. He peers over to look at my tablet. "What're you reading?" he asks.

"Another article about the *Grace Falls* anniversary," I reply. "Drink your milk."

"How many articles have they written about Mom?" he asks, still reading over my shoulder.

"A lot," I answer. "And I've been tasked to read all of them."

"Wow," Andy says, concentrating on the article, "so, the last time you were in a movie, Mom, you were thirty years old?"

"Now how did you figure that out?" Abby asks, buttering her toast.

"Well, it says here you stopped acting when I was born, and you're forty-three," he replies. "So that means you were thirty when you stopped acting?"

"You could also say I was thirty years old when you were born," Abby counterpoints. "I didn't exactly stop acting. I was just not playing the main roles like I was when I was younger. I wanted to spend more time raising you. But if you're going to do math like that, I expect to see good grades on your next math quiz."

"So are we going to this movie premiere?" Andy asks after taking a gulp of his milk. "Are Uncle Mason and Uncle Thomas going too?"

"You don't want to go to this one," Abby responds, joining the two of us at the counter. "It's just going to be a bunch of people pretending to like me for a few hours, which you never like to see."

"But I want to go to a fancy party!" Andy protests.

"Finish your milk and get ready for school," I say, turning off my tablet and finishing my coffee.

"Well, if I can't go to the party, will you get me a drawing tablet instead?" Andy tries to bargain.

"How about you do some more chores around the house, and we'll consider it," I answer. "We're leaving for school in five minutes."

Andy

"Alright, pencils down, class," Mr. Castro says with a cheeky smile. A few of my classmates laugh as we all put away our colored pencils. "So, who would like to show their posters first?"

Mr. Castro had us design movie posters in art class today. We are learning about composition—basically, how to make things stand out and where to put things in the picture to create what Mr. Castro calls "balance." He said if we couldn't think of something original to draw, we could try and recreate a poster we already knew, but we have to explain the composition of it.

From where I'm sitting, I look around at what everyone has drawn. I'm mostly sitting near guys in my class, and I can see they all drew some kind of superhero movie poster. Some of them almost look like they were trying to draw themselves as the superhero. I'd decided to try and draw a poster for a short story Dad wrote when I was little called "Magic and Madness" about a bunch of kids who discover a book they think is full of magic spells, but none of the magic works and it drives them crazy. It was one of my favorite stories growing up, and it isn't a movie, so there is no movie poster for it. Mom has a collection of movie posters that we used to look at a lot, some from movies she was in, but mostly movies she just really likes. I think, since Mr. Castro is teaching us about "balance" and "composition," that I should go back and look at them and see if I can see if the poster designs were really balanced. I wonder if I would recognize it?

Several of my classmates show off their posters first. I never like to volunteer to show my stuff. I still don't like talking in front of a group. Most of the boys in the class did draw superhero or action-adventure movie posters, and many of the girls drew romantic movie posters, though a few drew action comedies. Everyone does their best to explain the "balance" of their poster, but for the most part, everyone points out that, if they have two characters on the left side, they also have two characters on the right.

When I do finally show my poster, I can't explain if it's balanced or not. "It just looks right to me," I say.

Mr. Castro gives me a thumbs up for my effort.

"And finally, how about you, Miss Harper?" Mr. Castro asks the new girl in the class. I've never seen her before. I think she started just today. She wasn't in any of my other morning classes. "I know you weren't here when we started learning about composition, but let's see what you got!" Mr. Castro is always so encouraging.

"Here," the new girl says shyly, holding up her poster.

I definitely recognize the poster as one that Mom has in her collection. Several people turn to me and giggle after they see the name of the poster. I pull my hood over my head. I wish my hood was a foot longer to hide my whole face.

"Um..." the girl starts, obviously confused. "What's wrong?"

Mr. Castro answers warmly, "You can ask Mr. Bennett after class. I'm sure he'll be happy to explain why the class is acting so rudely."

Most everyone stops looking at me and turns back to the front of the classroom.

"I love the way you shaded the wings on your poster, Miss Harper," Mr. Castro says. "Good job."

Mr. Castro collects all our posters and says he's going to pick a few he thinks show good composition to hang in the classroom for a while. Class lets out soon after that, and I hurry out to get my sketchbook and lunch from my locker. Part of me wants to get away before I have to talk to that new girl and explain that the poster she drew is a movie that my mom starred in.

Everyone in my middle school knows who my mom is, but thankfully, no one really gives me a hard time about it anymore. I figure it's because most people don't care, or at least are nice enough to not bring it up. I only have a few classmates who were also in my class in fifth grade and were there for my antler freak-out. I thought that day would actually make my classmates more afraid of me, but instead, I became kinda popular. They tell their friends that they were there when "Andy grew his epic antlers and scared Bruno's dad," and then they got to meet the famous movie star, Abby Andrews. I was relieved that no one teased or bullied me after all that, but I didn't make too many friends either. I don't mind that, though. I like keeping to myself and drawing.

I usually have lunch in Mr. Castro's classroom so I can use the art supplies, and he can help me work on my drawing skills. I'll never tell the class, but I actually want to try and draw a picture of my mom in her angel movie as a gift to her to celebrate the anniversary. I asked Dad if she would like that as a gift. Dad said she would probably treasure it forever. That sounds like something Dad would say.

I grab my lunch bag and sketchbook and go back to Mr. Castro's room. When I enter, I see him still talking to the new girl from class. She is holding her glasses and seems to be showing him her cheeks for some reason. That's a little weird. Mr. Castro sees me come in and waves me over.

"Mr. Bennett," he says with a big smile on his face, "come over here and meet Miss Harper. Joslyn, this is Mr. Andy Bennett."

I walk into the room and reach out my hand to the new girl. "Hey," I say. "Nice to meet you."

"Thank you," she replies, putting her glasses back on and shaking my hand. "Nice to meet you too."

"I bet if you ask Mr. Bennett nicely," Mr. Castro says, "he'll tell you why everyone pointed at him when you showed your poster."

I shoot Mr. Castro a nasty look. He just winks at me.

"I'm going to grab my lunch. I'll be right back. You two introduce yourselves."

Mr. Castro goes into the back of the classroom where his office is. Me and the new girl just stand there looking at each other. It's super awkward.

"So..." Joslyn starts, clasping her hands behind her, and swaying back and forth, "did you like my poster?"

Not exactly the question I'm expecting. "Um..." I start, "sure. I, uh, liked the colors on the wings too. And I like how you got the shape of the letters to look like the real movie poster."

"Yeah," Joslyn replies. "*Grace Falls* is one of my favorite movies. I know it's kinda old for me, but I still like it."

"Cool...cool," I respond. I scratch the top of my head trying to think of something to say. I look closely at Joslyn. She's nice looking. Her glasses are a nice purple and make her eyes look wide. I try to see if she is wearing any eye makeup, which Mom says is a way for people to make their eyes look bigger, but she's not. Actually, it doesn't look like she's wearing any makeup at all. Nothing on her eyes, or cheeks, or lips. I think I like that better than the other girls in class who like to wear a lot of makeup. "I, uh, like your curly hair," I say. "It kinda looks like soft springs." That definitely sounded better in my head. I can feel my cheeks grow hot as I break eye contact.

"Thank you." She giggles. "I like my hair too."

Just then Mr. Castro comes out of his office with his lunch bag. "So," he says, "did Mr. Bennett tell you his connection to your poster?" Of course, he has to ask that question.

"No?" Joslyn replies, obviously confused.

Mr. Castro looks at me with a smile and a wink again.

I let out a heavy sigh. "I guess you'll find out anyways," I say, scratching my head again. "My mom is Abby Andrews. She was the star in *Grace Falls*."

Joslyn's wide eyes grow huge. "Your mom?" she asks excitedly. She starts blushing, which I can see really well since she's not wearing makeup.

I can't keep eye contact again. I don't know why, but I feel extra embarrassed by her reaction. I think I'm afraid if I keep looking at her, I'll just stare at her pink cheeks.

"Miss Harper, you don't want to be late for lunch," Mr. Castro interjects. "You should go now before the lines get too long."

"Oh!" she exclaims, looking at the clock. "Thank you for talking to me, Mr. Castro." Joslyn then turns to me with a big goofy smile. "Nice to meet you, Andy." Joslyn grabs her bag and hurries out of the classroom.

"Did I embarrass you?" Mr. Castro asks, sitting down at the table and unpacking his lunch.

"Yeah, a little," I reply. I don't mind being honest with Mr. Castro. He doesn't make me feel bad for it like some of my classmates do. "It's okay, though. She seems nice. And everyone gets excited when they hear about my mom. She'll get over it."

I turn around to get my lunch and sketchbook from the other table when I notice something on the ground near the door. It looked like a small tube of paint or something, but not like the tubes of paint we use in class.

I pick it up and read the label. Coral All-Natural Foundation - N51 Amber Honey. It's foundation makeup. It kinda looks like Joslyn's skin color. Did Joslyn drop this?

Wait, Joslyn *does* where makeup. But why only foundation? Why not anything else?

2

The Boy Who Gave the Girl Advice

Joslyn

I started at my new middle school a week ago and already I've met someone kinda famous! Momma and Daddy said I might when they decided to put me at this school. We moved into our new house last September, and I didn't like the public school I was first going to. Too many people started to pick on me. Momma didn't like that either, so they enrolled me in my new school. I'd never gone to a private school before. At first, I didn't want to go to a private school, because I thought I would have to wear a uniform or something, but there was no uniform for this school. It's only been a week, and I'm not sure how much I fit in, but no one has started making fun of me so far.

When that boy, Andy, found my makeup and gave it back to

me, I was really scared he was going to ask me why I had to use makeup, but he didn't ask. He just gave it back to me and smiled. I like Andy for that. He seems very nice. And I like his smile. Plus, I found out his mom is one of my most favorite actresses in the whole world! When I told Momma and Daddy about that, they just thought that must have been so neat. They wanted to know if I talked to him more and learned more about what he was like, but I didn't. I was too nervous to ask. We only just met on Monday, and we only have the one class together, Advanced Art. Andy is so nice and a super good artist, I don't want to really bother him.

Momma asks me if I've made any other friends at school yet, but I really haven't. I'm still sitting alone at lunch, but I'm okay with that. I like reading my books when I have lunch. Plus, if people don't get too close, they won't notice my face. I'm super afraid to get picked on again. Those kids at the other school were super nasty. I felt like I wanted to cry every day, but I didn't want to tell my parents. They were very busy unpacking our house, and Daddy was starting his new job. But I feel a little better now at my new school. I like most of my teachers and a lot of my classmates I've gotten to talk to so far seem nice too.

Momma makes her chicken and greens for dinner that night, one of my favorites. She hasn't gotten a lot of chances to cook in her new kitchen since we moved, as she has been working late shifts at the hospital, but she has the night off tonight. I don't really like when Daddy makes dinner. He mostly only knows how to boil hot dogs.

"So tell us about your first week," Daddy says as we start eating. "Do you still like your new school?"

"I do!" I say excitedly. "I like all my classes. The science lab is way better than at my old school. It's brighter and way cleaner. We're learning writing in English class, and I was asked to write a 250-word essay about me and read it to class if I wanted."

"Oh?" Momma asks, looking intrigued. "Did you actually read your essay out loud to the class?"

I go silent and look down at my plate. "I chickened out at the last minute," I say sadly. "But the teacher read it and said she liked it. She said I should think about sharing it with the class since I don't have any classmates that are biracial, and she thought the class might find that part about me really interesting."

"I bet they would," Daddy adds encouragingly. "Maybe I can come to pick you up and talk like Granddad with an Irish accent."

"Daddy!" I exclaim in horror. "Don't!"

"I'm kidding," he says with a mischievous smile.

"I hate your Irish accent," I retort, getting angry. "It's embarrassing."

"That's why I'm kidding!" Daddy replies, trying to defend himself.

"I don't believe you," I say back.

"That's enough, you two," Mom says, tapping her fork on her water glass. "Now, let's say grace so we can eat."

The rest of dinner is pretty normal, with Momma and Daddy mostly talking about work and stuff to do around the house. There is a lot they want to repair and some other things they want to renovate. That's why Momma's working later and longer shifts, so they could afford the work. Momma and Daddy don't get to spend a lot of time together with Momma's schedule, either, so they like to talk a lot at dinner. I try very hard to listen, but I don't understand what Daddy does very well, and Momma is a nurse and doesn't always like to tell me about what happens during her shifts.

I finish my dinner and excuse myself from the table so I can wash my face and put my pajamas on. When both Momma and Daddy are home on a Friday night, we do a movie night. Daddy got to pick tonight, and he wants to see one of the new action movies with all the fancy cars driving through buildings and crashing into planes and stuff. He loves those movies a whole lot, and admittedly Momma and I find them fun too.

I go into my bathroom, which is the one in the hall, and I get out my face soap and wet my face sponge. The sponge I had was getting all grimy and was almost the color of my makeup. I should remember to ask Momma to get me another one from her bathroom. I put the soap on my face and start to scrub my cheeks hard. The tan makeup I wear washes off, and I can see all my light and white spots on my cheeks. I do the same on my neck and jaw before wiping all the excess soap and water off. I look back and forth at my cheeks. Twelve spots. I still have twelve white spots on my face and neck. I always count the spots to make sure I've gotten off all the makeup.

I've had these spots on my face since I was seven years old, and I've always hated them. If I could hide them forever, I would. But I made a promise to Momma and Daddy that, when we are home, and it's just the three of us, that I would clean my face and walk around without makeup. Momma wants me to be less and less self-conscious of my skin, because, she says, it's unique and beautiful. Daddy, too, always says my face is cuter than even Momma's when I smile without my makeup.

I don't see it.

All those spots are too distracting. If I was looking at me, I think I wouldn't be able to concentrate. I wouldn't be able to hear what I was saying or anything. Or even worse, I wouldn't even *want* to look at me.

I don't know how, but Mr. Castro actually noticed that I was wearing makeup, and for some reason, I felt comfortable telling him why. Well, sort of. I told him my natural skin was a couple different colors and the makeup helps to make it just one color. He said he thought I did a good job making it look even, which is what Momma taught me to do when I was first learning to put it on. I wonder if Mr. Castro knows how to do makeup or something. After all, we live in an area with a lot of people who work in movies and TV and stuff. Maybe he's also a makeup artist or something.

I clean myself up, put on my pajamas, and go to the family room to wait for Daddy to start the movie. Momma's making popcorn, while Daddy's scrolling through Netflix to find it. I sit on the couch next to him and watch him click through the movies. I noticed, as he's scrolling through the recommended list, he passes by my favorite movie, *Grace Falls*. The picture is the same as the poster I tried to draw on Monday.

"Hey!" I exclaim, pointing to the screen. "That's my picture! I drew those wings in art class this week. Andy said he liked how I drew them."

"Oh, he did, did he?" Daddy responds, sounding impressed. "Well, maybe if you're lucky, you'll be able to show them to his mom someday."

I curl up in my seat, bringing my knees up to cover my face.

Daddy chuckles. "I'm sorry, sweetie," he says, putting an arm around me. "I really don't mean to embarrass you. I only say things like that because I love you and I'm very proud of you."

"I know, Daddy," I say. "And I love you too."

Rick

When Abby was on the press junket for *Grace Falls* twenty years ago, the studio went all out. They hired a private jet to take her and other members of the cast practically all over the world to promote the movie. I was only able to fly with her once. I had finished up a project and finalized a few items for our wedding and decided I would meet up with her at her last stop in Tokyo as a bit of a surprise (with Walter's help). I remember thinking, in my author's/hopeless romantic's mind that this would be the truest test of our future relationship together. Was she going to be overjoyed to see me, or was she going to be annoyed that I'd left my post and traveled halfway around the world for only a few days. I was so caught up in the thought that I could barely enjoy my flight over to Japan. The seat in coach didn't help matters.

To my tremendous relief, Abby was very happy. She wouldn't let me leave her side the rest of the trip. And I was reminded I never wanted to leave her side again.

And so, here we are in first class, on a flight together to New York for a few interviews and late-night talk show appearances. This flight, however, is going to be far from romantic. While Abby is doing her best to have a restful flight, I pore over her schedule repeatedly, double-checking every list of requirements. If I'm going to act as Abby's assistant for this press tour, I vowed to myself, I'm going to go above and beyond. Or at least above and beyond my self-perceived capabilities.

The lists of topics for most of the interviews are practically the same: "What was it like working on the movie?" "How long did you prepare for the wing-growing scene?" "How was it working with Director Kellin Ellis?", etc. Even so, each interviewee wants to pick out something that will help them stand out from the rest. A few of the late-night shows propose doing a bit or a sketch parodying the movie. Others want to find a niche moment in Abby's life to focus on for a good conversation. As I read through each brief and list of questions, one, in particular, pops out at me.

"Hey, honey," I say, tapping Abby on the arm to get her attention.

She takes off her headphones and leans over to me.

"I don't know if you read through these questions yet, but did you see this one asking about your physical health after the shoot? Have you ever talked about that before in any interviews?"

"Interesting," Abby says, looking at the list from my tablet. "Y'know, I'm not sure it's really ever come up in an interview. Huh. I guess I didn't realize that, since so many other people have written or speculated what it must have been like."

"I kinda think you should talk about this," I say in all seriousness. "I think it's important to share how dangerous it was and how you've had back problems practically ever since."

"I dunno," she replies with trepidation. "I mean, I could, but there's a lot more to it than just the back stuff, y'know? And I don't know that I want to open that can of worms. I honestly just want to get this whole big thing over with."

"Maybe it's *time* to open that can of worms," I offer. "I mean, you were practically forced into a contract that Mason easily got out of, so he didn't have to naturally produce huge wings like they originally wanted. You were overworked for eight hours, well past what you were told would be healthy for you. Hell, Ellis didn't even thank you when he accepted his Oscar for Best Director for the damn movie! You practically *made* the movie for him with your work!"

"Okay, okay," Abby says, taking my arm and calming me down. "While I think your last comments are debatable, I will admit that talking about the work hours and the unfair contract negotiations are worth addressing. But..."

"But what?" I ask, concerned.

"I don't know that I want to be the poster child for those things," she replies honestly. "I'm not entirely comfortable with that idea. I mean, if someone else started the conversation, I guess I could contribute, but again, can of worms and all."

"I don't want to make you do anything you're not comfortable doing," I say, trying to comfort her. "In my opinion, I think you should at least consider taking out the can opener and putting it on the table."

Abby chuckles at that. I love making her laugh.

"And whatever you do," I add, "you have my support. One hundred percent."

"Thank you, my love," she says, giving me a loving peck on the cheek. "And I hope you know, you will always have mine."

God, I love this woman!

Andy

Mom and Dad left this morning to fly to New York for a few days while Mom does press for the rerelease of her movie, so Gramma Dee Dee is staying with me while they're away. And while Gramma makes the best breakfasts, she always forgets to make me lunch, so she gives me a few dollars, instead, to buy lunch. I get chicken nuggets and a chocolate milk lunch. As I go to leave, so I can get to Mr. Castro's classroom, I see Joslyn sitting by herself at a small table in the back corner of the cafeteria. I feel like I should go check on her. I don't know why. Just seems like a nice thing to do.

I turn and walk toward her table. She's reading a book and eating a sandwich. I stand by her table for a second to see if she looks up. She doesn't.

"Hey," I say kinda quietly, kinda loud, getting her attention.

Joslyn looks up from her book startled.

"I'm sorry," I say, a little embarrassed. "I didn't mean to scare you."

"Oh," she says, smiling shyly, "hi, Andy. I didn't see you. How're you doing?"

"I'm good," I say, nodding. "My parents are out of town, so my gramma is staying with me." Why did I share that? "Um, how're you doing? You're sitting here all by yourself?"

"Oh, I'm fine," she answers. "I'm just reading. Um, are you looking for a place to sit?"

"I..." That same something that said I should check on her tells me I should sit down for just a second. "Um, yeah. Can I sit with you?"

"Sure," she replies happily. She moves her lunch closer to her to make room for my tray. I sit down in the chair across from her and set down my lunch. "Are you not having lunch in Mr. Castro's room today?"

"Um, well, yeah. That is, I might go back to his room in a minute. I don't normally buy my lunch, but my parents are out of town, and my gramma is staying with me." *You already told her that*, I scold myself in my head. Why am I so weird talking to her? "So, what are you reading?"

"Oh," she says, turning the book over. "It's called *The Sisters Travel*. It's about these three sisters who run away from their home in Virginia and want to get to California any way they can."

"Ah," I say. "Is it good?"

"Yeah, I like it," Joslyn says. "Do you like any books?"

"Not really," I reply. "I mean, I totally read!" *Why did I say that?* I scream in my head. "I mean, I don't read a lot of books. I'll read some of my dad's books sometimes, but he writes more stuff for younger children now. I like comic books, though."

"I always thought comic books were kinda scary," Joslyn says.

"Oh, not all of them!" I say. "Like, they have comics about younger kids as superheroes, who fight bad guys, and some based on cartoons and stuff like that."

"Ah," Joslyn says. "Cool."

We look at each other for a few seconds without saying anything. Joslyn breaks eye contact first and starts to glance away. She's still smiling though. She thinks I'm weird. I just know it.

"If you want," I say, "you could come with me to Mr. Castro's classroom. He lets some of his students hang out in his room for lunch if we want to work on our art projects, or want a quiet place to sit. You don't have to if you don't want to!"

"Um," Joslyn says, looking at the table, "I...um...sure. Yeah. I can have lunch in Mr. Castro's classroom with you."

Awesome! I think to myself. Wait, why is this awesome? Why does this make me happy?

"Cool," I say. "Let's go!"

Joslyn packs her remaining lunch back in her bag, grabs her things, and walks with me to Mr. Castro's classroom. *Maybe I shouldn't have invited her*, I think to myself. Maybe she was comfortable in her spot. And I made her pack up her stuff just to go to a room away from people. Man, that was so rude. Maybe I should apologize.

Mr. Castro's sitting in his usual spot at one of the worktables, eating his salad and reading from his phone when we walk in. "Oh look!" he exclaims as we enter. "You brought a friend! I'm so glad you could join us, Miss Harper."

I feel embarrassed again for a second. I didn't bring her; I made her come. She didn't have to come with me. I look over at Joslyn. She's smiling, which makes me feel a little better. Maybe I didn't make her come. Maybe she actually wanted to come.

I put my school lunch on the worktable and sit across from Mr. Castro like I usually do. Joslyn pulls out the chair next to me and sits down. I wasn't expecting her to join us; I figured she was going to sit at another table and read again. But I'm actually kinda happy that she's sitting next to me instead.

Joslyn drops her backpack on the ground and several items roll out. She quickly jumps out of her seat to collect them. I jump down to help her. I see her makeup tube roll under the table, so I crawl under and grab it for her.

"Here you go," I say, handing it back to her.

She quickly grabs it from my hand and shoves it deep into her bag. "Thank you," she says quietly, looking at the floor.

Had I done something wrong? "I'm sorry," I say.

"Oh, no!" Joslyn quickly says. "No, you didn't do anything wrong. I just...I don't like anyone knowing I wear makeup."

"Why is that weird?" I ask. "It's just foundation. A lot of girls wear it, right?"

Joslyn just keeps looking at the ground. She's fidgeting nervously.

I look over to Mr. Castro for help. He's just watching us, looking curious. I get the feeling he wants to say something, but he also wants to stay out of it.

I look back at Joslyn. "I don't think it's weird," I say. "When my mom was a kid, she was in movies and on TV, and she told me she wore makeup all the time."

"That's...not why I wear makeup," she responded quietly. "I..."

"Oh?" I reply a little confused. I start to feel super bad talking about it. It's clearly making her uncomfortable, and I really don't want to make her uncomfortable. Then she might want to leave, and I don't want her to leave. "It's okay. You wear makeup. No big deal. It's not weird. Or, at least, I don't think it's weird."

I try to smile, thinking maybe it will make her feel better. She just keeps looking down. How can I make her look up again? Then I think of something.

"Oh! You wanna see what I'm working on?" I run over to one of the cubbies in the corner of the classroom where Mr. Castro stores our work. I pull out the poster I'm working on for Mom. Since Joslyn likes this movie, maybe she'll like to see my poster, I think. Maybe it will make her feel better.

I bring it over to one of the other tables and take off the tracing paper that's protecting it. Joslyn comes over and looks at my poster. Her eyes grow wide like last time.

"Wow," she says, amazed. "It looks exactly like the movie poster."

"I want it to be a present for my mom," I say. "She's been super busy lately, and I thought this might be a nice present for her when her movie comes out again next month. I know you like her movie too. What do you think?"

Joslyn looks at my poster for what feels like a long time without saying anything. I start to feel nervous. Is there something wrong with it? Does she actually not like it?

Finally, she looks up at me with a big smile, bigger than I've seen her have before. "It's awesome," she says, sounding very impressed. "I love it!"

"Thanks," I say gratefully. I look over at Mr. Castro. He smiles and gives me a wink.

Joslyn

Andy invited me to sit next to him in our art class the day after he showed me the poster he was working on. He offered to help me with my art projects if I got stuck or something. That is super nice of him. Plus, I get to see his smile, which makes me very happy for some reason. He sits at a table with mostly boys, but it doesn't bother me so much, because I'm sitting next to Andy.

Before class starts, he shows me some of his drawings in his sketchbook. He is an amazing drawer. He likes to draw animals.

Some of them look very realistic, while others look like cartoons. He's really good at drawing both, I think.

The classwork for today involves mixing paint colors. Mr. Castro's teaching us how to tell if a color is warm or cool. "Warm colors," he explained, "will look like they have more yellow or orange or red in them, while cool colors look like they have more blues and blue-ish purples. What I want you to do is take the three primary colors and mix three warm colors and three cool colors, and then use those colors and paint swatches on your paper." He asks if we have any questions and everyone shakes their heads, so we all start mixing paints.

I try to mix cool colors first and want to make a purple. Andy warns me that red paint can be very red when you mix it with other colors, so you don't need more than a little drop. He's right! I mix way more red than I thought, and the purple almost looks like a dark red. I think Momma calls the color burgundy or something. She has a pair of scrubs this color.

While Andy's helping me mix colors, the boys across from us at the table start dipping their brushes in paint and flicking it to make it spray out and onto the table. It's really annoying, but I try to ignore it and just focus on the assignment. Then the guys start to see how far they could flick the paint with just their brushes, spreading out their papers on the table to try and measure the distance. Mr. Castro catches this and warns them to stop. I feel a little better and think that will stop them from messing around, so I go back to painting my swatches.

I paint a green swatch, and when I look at it, I can't tell if it was warm or cool. I think it looks more yellow than blue, which would make it warm, but maybe the light was making it look more yellow. I look up to ask Andy what he thinks, when all of a sudden, a splash of red paint splatters all over my right glasses lens.

I screech at the shock, and everyone turns around.

The boys stop and immediately put down their brushes.

"Oh, my bad," one of them says, getting out of his chair and stepping away from the table.

"Mr. Collins, Mr. Rodriguez," Mr. Castro scolds, "apologize to Miss Harper and clean up the table."

"Yes sir," they said quietly. "Sorry." That's all they say before they hurry over to the counter to get paper towels.

Andy leans over to check on me. "You okay?" he asks. He sounds kinda worried. "Did you get any in your mouth?"

I don't think so, but I instinctively reached my hand to my face to check. Oh no! Not only did they get paint on my glasses, but it's on my face too!

"Mr. Castro," Andy says, raising his hand, "Joslyn got paint on her face. Can she go to the bathroom and clean it up?"

That's so nice of him to ask for me, I think. I wonder if he really is worried.

"Of course," Mr. Castro says, and gives me a hall pass.

I get out of my chair and walk out of the classroom and down the hall a bit to the girls' bathroom. I look at myself in the mirror. They got paint on my glasses, my cheek, my chin, and the collar of my shirt. How the heck did they do that? I wet a paper towel, put some hand soap on it, and start to wipe off my cheeks first. I can't tell if I'm washing the paint or just smearing it. I scrub a little harder just in case. I check the paper towel. I've scrubbed the paint off...but also my makeup.

I quickly wipe off the soap to see if maybe I only wiped off a little. My cheek is white. Maybe that's just leftover soap. I wipe again. I look at the paper towel. More makeup!

What do I do? I can't go back into the classroom like this! They'll see my real skin! And they'll make fun of me! Andy will make fun of me! I don't want Andy to make fun of me! Would I be able to sneak back into the classroom and get my makeup and then make an excuse to go back out again? Why hadn't I thought to bring my makeup with me? This was the worst thing I could do!

I start to cry. I'm so embarrassed. How can I hide my face? I'm starting to think it'd be better if I just covered my face in red paint than show my real skin. Maybe I'll be able to hide my face with my hair and go back into the classroom. I'll just keep my hair in my face, get my bag, and ask Mr. Castro if I can go to the bathroom again. He'll let me do that. I could do that. I can do that. It'll be quick. And no one will see my face.

I leave the bathroom and keep my head down, making sure my hair is hanging in front of my face while I walk back down the hall. Mr. Castro's class is the last one on the left.

I can get there without having to look up. I walk carefully, staring at the gold line between the floor tiles. At the classroom, I open the door to everyone still talking and chatting, while they continue painting. No one notices I'm back.

I keep my head down and walk around the edge of the class-room, staring at the floor. All I needed to do was get to the table in the corner and get my bag. I can do that. I can do that.

Suddenly, I run into someone. "Ow!" they exclaim.

Out of instinct, I look up to apologize. It's one of the boys who flung paint at me. He's holding a paint-covered paper towel.

"Hey! Wait, what happened to your face?"

Oh no! Not again...

Other kids turn around.

"Whoa," another kid says. "What's wrong with your skin?"

I start to cry. *Not again. Not again.*

"Yeah," yet another kid says, "what happened to your face? Are you sick, or something?"

I feel tears rolling down my cheeks. It's all happening again. I can't do it. I can't do it.

"Hey!"

Everyone goes silent. I look over. Everyone's looking at Andy.

"Leave her alone!" he demanded. "That's just what her face looks like, and there's nothing weird about that, okay?"

He gets out of his chair and kneels down behind the table for a few seconds before getting back up and hurrying over to me. He gets up close and discreetly hands me my makeup. "At least, *I* don't think it's weird," he says with a smile. "And you shouldn't either."

I'm still crying, but this time it's because what Andy said to me made me very happy.

3

The Girl Who Tried and the
Boy Who Cried

Rick

"Oh, that is very kind of you! Thank you. Let me consult with my better half, and I'll let you know. ... No, thank you for the invitation. And thank you for letting me know. ... Absolutely, I will tell her. ... Yes. Thank you again. Goodbye."

I hang up my cell phone and walk from my office to the living room, where Abby is lying down on the couch. It has been two days since we got back from New York, and Abby's legacy back pains started acting up.

"I just had the most wonderful phone call," I say to her, sitting on the floor face to face with Abby.

"Oh?" she says with curiosity.

"You know that young girl, Joslyn, that Andy talked about

from his art class?" I ask. "Well, that was her mother. She invited us over to their place tomorrow for lunch, to thank Andy for standing up for Joslyn in their art class the other day."

"Oh, that's wonderful," Abby says with the smile of a proud mother.

"Apparently, the kids in class were talking about Joslyn and making her feel uncomfortable, and Andy told everyone to knock it off and leave her alone," I explain. "And they wanted me to tell you that they absolutely appreciate your son for what he did."

"Aww, that's so sweet," Abby replies lovingly. She's clearly getting emotional. "That is exactly what I wanted to hear today. Tell them I appreciate their compliment, and we're proud of him too. You should take Andy over there tomorrow and meet them. They would appreciate that."

"I'll take it up with Andy first," I say. "And I did want to check and see if you wanted to come, but I'll leave that up to you."

"I very much doubt I'll be able to move at all this weekend." Abby sighs. "Did you watch it? The interview on *The Late Show*?"

I take a breath and compose myself. "I know what you're asking," I start, "and you know I'm going to say you absolutely did the right thing. I spoke with both Walter and Mason afterward, and they couldn't be more proud of you. Mason even said he would address the same thing during his appearance on *The Late Show* tonight."

"Can we pretend for a little while that everything's normal?" Abby asks, as tears start to fill her eyes.

I lean over and give her a soft kiss on her forehead. "Everything is going to be fine," I assure her. "I promise. And everything is normal and wonderful. *And* your son's a hero, protecting the cute, vulnerable girl in his class."

"Just like his father," Abby replies with a gentle smile.

Andy

Dad and I pull up in front of Joslyn's house. Dad starts to exit the car, but for some reason, I can't move.

He sits back down and closes the door, looking at me with concern. "What's wrong?" he asks. "Everything alright, bud?"

"I don't know why," I say, "but I just got nervous. Like, this is kinda weird."

"Do you not want to stay?" he asks. "We can go in for a short time and excuse ourselves early if you'd like."

"No!" I say quickly. "I do want to stay. I just...I dunno. I was thinking today that, maybe...do you think they really wanted to do this to thank me?"

"Why else would they?" Dad asks.

"I dunno," I say. "Because they wanted to meet Mom?"

"Ah," Dad says, nodding. "I understand. You don't want this to be another one of those things. I get that. For what it's worth, when I told Mrs. Harper that Mom wasn't going to be able to come, she said she completely understood and that she hoped you were still coming over, because she was looking forward to meeting you."

"Did she really say that?" I ask.

"She absolutely did," Dad replies, smiling. "And I really got the feeling they wanted to do this for you."

"I didn't do much," I say, shrugging a little. "I just didn't want to see Joslyn cry is all."

"And for a parent, that can be everything," Dad says. "Let's go in. And whenever you want to leave, you let me know."

Dad's words make me feel better. I get out of my car and retrieve our "contribution to the lunch," as Dad called it—Mom's favorite potato salad from our favorite deli. We walk up to the door, and Dad rings the doorbell. Joslyn's dad opens the door. I recognize him from when he picked her up from school the day her shirt got stained from the paint attack. He's wearing a clean polo shirt with the logo of one of the local phone and internet companies. I didn't notice how red his hair was in the light.

"Hello!" he greets us enthusiastically. "You must be the young man who saved my daughter."

"Daddy!" we hear a voice scream in the house. Joslyn pushes her dad out of the doorway. "Sorry. My dad's the worst. Come in."

I look up at Dad like I'm looking for permission or a second opinion. Dad just smiles and gently pushes me through the doorway. Joslyn closes the door, and our dads shake hands and formally introduce themselves to each other.

"I'm Rick," Dad says.

"David," Mr. Harper replies. "Wonderful to meet you. We've heard amazing things about your son."

"And we of your daughter," Dad says.

I look over at Joslyn. I can't tell if she's embarrassed or happy. She's definitely blushing. Just then, Joslyn's mom comes out of the kitchen wearing a well-worn blue apron, wiping her hand on a dishrag before reaching her hand to my dad.

"Hi. Monica," she greets. "Lovely to meet you." She then looks at me with a very bright smile. "And you're Andy? So lovely to meet you too."

"Thank you, Mrs. Harper," I reply. I hold up the bag with the potato salad containers. "We wanted to bring something for lunch. This is my mom's suggestion. I hope you like potato salad."

"Oh, that's so thoughtful," Mrs. Harper says happily, taking the bag from me. "We love potato salad! Lunch will be ready shortly. Why don't you boys have a seat in the living room. Joslyn and I will let you know when everything's ready."

Joslyn puts on a proud grin. "Momma's making her famous pan-fried chicken for lunch," she says to us. "And I'm making cornbread!"

"Sounds amazing," Dad replies. "Can't wait."

"Yeah," I say. "I love cornbread." That wasn't untrue, but I still think that may've sounded weird to say.

Joslyn's smile grows bigger. I hoped that means she's happier and not that she was trying to keep herself from laughing at my weird comment.

Mr. Harper leads us into their living room. Dad and I sit on their couch, while Mr. Harper sits on another chair off to the side. He rotates the chair a bit to face us more. Dad asks Mr. Harper how long they've been living there, assuming, since Joslyn is so new to the school, they must have moved recently. Mr. Harper explains they moved several months ago when he got a new job in the city. He tells us he's a data scientist. I don't know what that means, but Dad seems to know. They talk about statistics and reading dashboards. I have no idea how my dad know what a data scientist does. Did he research the job for a book or project? He does that on occasion and then talks about it to Mom and me over dinner, sometimes several dinners.

I feel myself zoning out and just looking around the room. The Harpers have several pictures on a table near the front window. One is a wedding photo from Mr. and Mrs. Harper's wedding. They're standing in front of a church altar, with candles on it, and two huge flower arrangements on either side of them. Next to that photo is a picture of people I assume are Mrs. Harper's parents, as they are Black like Mrs. Harper. Next to that is a picture of Joslyn as a baby with, I think, her grandfather on her dad's side, since he's white like Mr. Harper. Joslyn was a really cute baby.

I keep looking around the living room. The couch faces the TV and TV stand, which is placed in front of a fireplace. That's a little weird to put the TV in front of the fireplace, but I guess they don't have another place to put the TV. The wall to the right has three bookshelves, one with different books and one with DVDs. The other has, well, random stuff stacked on the shelves. I wonder if they're still unpacking.

I'm so distracted by the room, I miss Mr. Harper's question until Dad nudges me with his elbow.

"What?" I say, startled.

"Mr. Harper asked how you like school," Dad says gently.

"Oh, school's fine," I say. "I mean, it's just school, I guess."

"Are you looking forward to high school?" Mr. Harper asks.

"I dunno," I reply. "But I am looking forward to learning how to drive," I add. That makes Mr. Harper and Dad laugh a little.

"Have you thought about what kind of car you'd like?" Mr. Harper asks.

"I don't know much about cars," I admit. "Mom and Dad

keep telling me they aren't going to buy me a car until I go to college."

"We tell Joslyn the same thing," Mr. Harper says with a chuckle. "Of course, I think she should consider taking her grandfather's old van. I keep telling her she should take it and turn it into a party van with lights and speakers and—"

"Daddy!" Joslyn screams at her dad from behind us. "Stop embarrassing me!"

"I'm sorry," Mr. Harper says with a smile. "For embarrassing you, not for wanting you to get Grampa's van. Is lunch ready, love?"

"Yep!" Joslyn says with a smile and a bounce. "Table's all set."

"Great!" Mr. Harper exclaims.

We follow Joslyn to the dining room. They have a round table, and it's comfortably set for five people. Mr. Harper asks what we want to drink. Dad sits next to me on my left and Joslyn sits on my right.

"So," Dad says leaning around me to talk to Joslyn, "I hear you like the movie, *Grace Falls.*"

I look up at my dad desperately. Why is he bringing up Mom's movie? I know it's all he's had to think about for the last couple months, but does he have to bring it up at lunch? Dad gives me a gentle smile, as if to assure me he knows what he's doing.

"Are you going to see it when they rerelease it in the theater?"

"Um," Joslyn says shyly, "yeah. I'd like to. But...um...Momma said I wasn't supposed to talk about that during lunch."

"Oh," Dad replies. "Well, if she asks, you can say I brought it up." Dad reaches into his shirt pocket and pulls out a small envelope. The back of it says "Joslyn." Dad hands it to her. "This is for you."

Joslyn opens the envelope as Mr. and Mrs. Harper come out of the kitchen holding dishes and bowls with chicken, cornbread, and potato salad. Dad nudges me and nods at our hosts. He wants us to help them set the table. We get up and take a few of the dishes from them to place on the table, while Mr. Harper goes back in to retrieve drinks. Mrs. Harper takes off her apron and throws it on the counter before taking a seat next to Joslyn.

I look over at Joslyn as I place the cornbread on the table. Is she...crying? Oh no! Is she alright?

"What do you have there?" Mrs. Harper asks Joslyn, leaning over to see what she's reading.

"It's a note to me from Abby Andrews," Joslyn says, a little choked up. She beams up at her mom. "And look! She signed a picture for me too!"

Mrs. Harper takes the picture and note and reads it carefully. She starts smiling too. "Oh, that is so nice of her," Mrs. Harper says gratefully. She looks over at me as I take my seat again. "Please tell your mom thank you for this very sweet note and the autograph."

"Oh, sure," I said. Mom doesn't often write notes and sign autographs for my friends or classmates. When she does write a note or give someone her autograph, it's really because she wants to.

"The card there is part of all the promotional material created for the movie rerelease," Dad explains. "I hope it doesn't make it less special when I say we are up to our knees in promotional stuff, but she wanted to give you something special, since she couldn't be here for lunch. She's been on the press circuit, and when she has a moment to rest, I make her take it."

That's very respectful of Dad to not bring up the whole reason Mom couldn't join us is because she has a really bad backache. Mom told me before we left that she really did want to come with us. I believe her too.

We pass the plates of food around and take portions from each dish. Mr. Harper pours out water and lemonade for everyone. Mrs. Harper then asks if it's okay if she says grace. We all bow our heads while Mrs. Harper blesses the meal and gives thanks for us being here to have lunch with them. She also says a blessing for Mom. At home, we only say grace on major holidays, like Thanksgiving and Christmas. When we're over at other people's houses and they say grace, sometimes I feel uncomfortable, like I don't believe that they mean what they're praying for. But when Mrs. Harper is saying grace, I really feel like she means it. That makes me happy. I'll have to tell Mom they mentioned her in grace. She'd like that. I peek over at Dad. He's smiling like he's thinking the same thing.

Lunch is delicious. Mrs. Harper's chicken is just crispy, not too hard or crunchy. And it's super juicy, like I like it. The cornbread is good too. Mr. Harper says he really likes the potato salad. He says his "Irish side" always appreciates potatoes in any form. The adults mostly talk about their jobs. Mrs. Harper is a nurse at one of the better hospitals in the area. Mr. Harper works at the internet provider company on his shirt. Dad talks about being Mom's personal assistant for the last month and how he's managing her schedule. Mr. Harper is very interested in what Dad's talking about, and he doesn't bring Mom up much at all. He says he's interested in logistics. Do data scientists need to know logistics too?

Eventually, Mrs. Harper asks me how I like art class. Joslyn had told her I was good at drawing and that I was helping her with the class assignments. I'm not very good at talking about my own artwork, but I tell Mrs. Harper that I'll show her my drawings next time I see her and have my sketchbook. This makes her happy. I look over at Joslyn. She's wearing her big smile again. I feel myself smiling too. I think I like making her happy.

We finish up lunch and Mrs. Harper says she's going to churn some ice cream for dessert and that it should be ready in about half an hour. "Why don't you two hang out in the sunroom," Mrs. Harper offers to me and Joslyn. "Jos has a bookshelf out there with her favorite books, and I think the tablets are charging out there if you want to play a game."

"Ooo, I have a game I've been wanting to play, if you want!" Joslyn exclaims excitedly.

I smile and nod, and we excuse ourselves.

Joslyn leads me through the kitchen to their back sunroom. It looks like it used to be an open porch that they just built walls around with thick plastic windows. They have a wicker couch with a colorful floral print against the back wall and lots of plants hanging from the ceiling and sitting on shelves. There's also a white bookshelf with lots of worn books that look like they could be Joslyn's.

I sit down on the couch and Joslyn retrieves two tablets plugged in on top of her bookshelf. Joslyn hands one to me. "Daddy is always getting new tablets from his job," she says. "He and Momma both have the newest ones, and they give me their old ones. That one is the third newest and this one is the oldest. Just click the button on the bottom to unlock it. I don't think there's a passcode on it anymore."

I click the button and the tablet turns on. It already has YouTube open and shows playlists from *The Late Show*. I notice the playlist at the top features Uncle Mason as the guest. The one before it has my mom's interview.

Joslyn sits down next to me and looks over. "Oh!" she screeches. "You weren't supposed to see that!" She reaches over to try and hit a button, but I pull the tablet out of her reach.

"No, it's okay," I say. "Were you watching these before? Was Mom good in the interview?"

"Oh..." Joslyn says, a little shy. "Um, yeah. It was good. Um, I didn't know all the stuff she was talking about in the interview. Did you see it?"

"No," I answer. "I don't really watch Mom's TV interviews. I'll watch when she's in a movie or something, but I always feel like she's not herself in interviews. Dad says she has to 'put on appearances' or something like that."

"Oh really?" Joslyn says a little puzzled. "Because in this inter-view she looked like she was going to cry."

"She was going to cry?" I say, surprised. I look at the video list and read the title of the interview. "Abby Andrews: Filming was so painful and I could never talk about it." What does that mean?

I tap on the video, and it loads very quickly. I hold up the tablet so we both can watch. I didn't mean to change our plans and watch this video, but Joslyn doesn't stop me. She sits a little closer to get a better look at the tablet.

The video opens with the host introducing Mom, listing off

a few of her more recognizable movies and roles. He then announces her by name, and Mom walks out across the stage. The host meets her just before she makes it to the desk and gives her a kiss on both cheeks. She turns to wave at the band before continuing to the seat next to the desk. The desk and seats are up a few steps, and the host helps Mom up the steps. Mom is wearing a light blue blouse and matching pants that flow like a skirt when she walks. She's also wearing a chunky red necklace and matching earrings that look like that might've belonged to Gramma at one time. Her hair is down but pulled back over her ears so we can see her face. Mom is actually very pretty when she's all made up. Is it weird to think your mom is pretty?

The host opens by thanking her for being on the show. Before the interview, he pulls up a picture he's gotten from social media of a selfie with her and Dad in Times Square, commenting on how happy she looks and asks if she liked New York in fall. Mom says she likes New York (I don't know if that's true or not) and how she and Dad spent the day just walking around sightseeing and trying different foods. The host seems very nice.

Then, the host talks about *Grace Falls*, starting with a quick description of the movie and listing off all the awards and accolades. He asks Mom how the press tour is going, which I think is an odd question. Why isn't he talking about the movie? Isn't that why Mom is there?

Then, he says something that really surprises me. "Now, originally both you and your costar, Mason Drake, were going to have scenes where you both grew wings, isn't that right?"

"Yes, the original script had both Grant and Celeste grow wings at the end," Mom explains.

"So then what happened to change that?" the host asks. "Was it a change in the script?"

"Not exactly," Mom says. She seems a little hesitant but continues. "Mason and I worked together on our techniques in prep for the transformation scene. We were working with two different Creators, and our Creators were working together."

"You, of course, worked with Walter Saint James," the host politely interjects, "and Mason worked with Jules LeGrande, correct?"

"Right," Mom agrees. "Jules and Walter were working with us and getting notes from the director, and once they realized the size and breadth of the wings, they became concerned that we would get injured if we even attempted it. So, Jules and Walter went to the director and producers with their concerns, and they came back with a rewrite and new contracts. Mason no longer had to transform wings, but I still did, though only for one shot, instead of my original two."

"So, even though there was concern for your safety, they still kept the one scene and had you under contract to perform the transformation?" the host clarifies.

"Correct," Mom answers. "I was still scripted and contractually obligated to grow wings on film, but only once, instead of for two separate scenes. They, instead, scheduled shooting for all those scenes that one day."

"So all scenes where you have your wings were all shot in the same day?"

"All in the same eight hours, yes," Mom replies. "As well as much of the promotional photography and photos for the posters. They basically milked every second they could out of those things." Mom puts on a smile at that line, but I can tell she isn't happy.

"Now, were you supposed to carry those wings for eight hours?" the host asks. "I'm not a Muse, but that seems like a lot of time for transformations so big."

"I was only supposed to keep them for six hours," Mom answers, "but reshoots happened to go longer than anticipated."

"Do you think they lied to you about only needing six hours?"

"I think the six-hour limit was actually the recommendation of the medical professionals. I think they would have shot as much as possible if no one set a limit."

"So, then, that must have been incredibly painful," the host comments with sincerity. "How did you get through all that?"

"Well," she starts, "besides the injections for pain management, I mostly spent my free moments talking about my upcoming nuptials with my now husband. He really did help keep my mind off that."

"Oh, how sweet," the host says with a kind smile. "Now, this movie won several awards, including writing and directing, but you didn't even get a nomination for your performance. How did that make you feel, considering you literally carried the movie on your back?"

Joslyn leans over and whispers to me, "This is the part. The part where it looks like she's going to cry."

"Well," Mom says carefully, "I know this is extremely cliché, but truly I work for the craft and not the awards. Even back then, I would rather have just been home in my pajamas than sitting through award ceremonies and all that crap."

The audience laughs at that line. Mom seems to take a breath, but her breath is like a stutter. Like she's crying but on the inside.

"But, specifically for this part, I remember, at the time, feeling more used than anything. I mean, let's be honest, if you measure the length of the movie, I'm in a good fifty-five minutes of it and only have wings for seven minutes. But that's all everyone talks about, all everyone sees on the posters, and—no offense—all everyone wants to talk about."

"I'm not offended at all," the host says kindly. "If you ask me, your best role was Madam Redstone, and you're not playing as a Muse in that part."

"Oh, thank you, that's very nice of you," Mom says with a smile. "But, to go back to your question, I did feel a little denied. And the wings actually did injure my back."

"Oh really," the host says, somewhat surprised.

"I actually have some rather ugly scars on my shoulder blades from them," Mom explains, "and now I don't wear open-back dresses or blouses, which weirdly, produces unusually harsh comments from fashion commentators. I remember thinking, how much skin do you need to see in order to find a piece of clothing attractive? Skin is where the clothing, y'know, *isn't*."

The audience has a big laugh at that.

But I don't want to laugh. I don't know what I'm feeling. Definitely sad. And angry. But who am I angry at? What am I angry at? I feel like I'm angry at...everything and everyone. Who thinks hurting someone just to make a movie is a good thing? And who would want to hurt my mom over hurting Uncle Mason? Why didn't anyone stop them? And now they're putting the movie out again so everyone can see Mom get hurt? Why would they do that?

And Dad was with her and didn't stop them either? Or Uncle Mason? Or Uncle Walter?

And how can Joslyn like this movie? What can she possibly like about this? What kind of person—

I turn off the tablet and give it back to Joslyn. I can't even look at her, I'm so upset. I get up from the seat and walk over to the window to hide my face, hide my feelings.

"Wait," Joslyn says from behind me.

I hear what sounds like her trying to collect the tablets and set them down before she gets up from the couch.

"What happened? Are you okay?"

"I didn't know that's what happened to my mom," I say, trying to contain myself. "It made me upset. I'm sorry."

"But you didn't see the end," Joslyn replies.

For some reason that response makes me super angry. I whip around to look at her. I must have startled her, as she takes a small step back.

"I don't care!" I say angrily. "How could you watch this stuff? How could you like this stuff? People got hurt making that movie. My *mom* got hurt!"

"But," Joslyn tries to say gently, "she said...um...she was fine..."

"So I don't know my own mom?" I exclaim. "Everyone thinks they know her because she's famous. And then they want to tell me about her. Or they want to be my friend because they want to meet her. But no one cares about her. Or me. And now she's telling people she was hurt on TV, and you still want to tell me you know better? I thought you wanted to be my friend for real!"

"I do," Joslyn says quietly. "I do want to be your friend. But..." She trails off, and I noticed she's no longer looking at me. Her eyes move to look above my head. Her jaw drops and her eyes grow wider.

Then I notice her slowly stepping backward. *Oh no. Not again. Not in front of her...*

I reach my hands to my head. I feel them. Two growths sprouting from the top of my head, split a few inches from the top. Hard like bone.

They grew back. Not again.

I have no words. I can't explain. I can't apologize. I can't say anything. All I want is to get away from there. I don't want her to see me like this. I didn't want her to know.

I'm so frightened and frantic, I can't find a door out of the sunroom. The only thing I can do is run out the front door. I don't stop to think. I sprint past Joslyn, run through the kitchen, through the dining room, past the living room, out the front door, and down the street. I let my legs take me away from Joslyn's house. I really don't care where I'm going, as long as it's far away.

Why did she have to see this? Why did I yell at her? She didn't do anything wrong.

Now she'll never want to talk to me again.

4

The Girl Who Gave the Boy Advice

Rick

"Andy!"

The Harpers and I are chatting in their living room when we hear Joslyn scream Andy's name, and we see him rush out the front door. I don't get a clear look before the door slams shut.

Joslyn comes running out of the kitchen as I hurry to the front door to see if I can catch up to him. By the time I get outside, he's running around the corner.

"What happened?" Monica asks, checking on Joslyn.

"I'm sorry," Joslyn begins to confess as she starts to cry. "I didn't mean to show him."

"Show him what, love?" Monica asks gently.

"He opened up my tablet," Joslyn explains through tears. "And he saw the video with Miss Andrews's interview. And he wanted to watch it. It made him upset and..."

"And what, love?"

"And then," Joslyn continues, wiping tears from her cheeks, "and then he started to grow antlers on his head. And he got scared and ran away. I'm sorry, Momma! I didn't mean to make him mad."

"Oh, baby," Monica says with great love and understanding. She gives Joslyn a big comforting hug.

I take a breath and pull out my phone to call Abby.

"Is everything all right?" David asks, concerned. "Should we go after him?"

"I think I know where he's going," I say. "Let me give my wife a call and let her know what happened." I turn to poor Joslyn, who is clearly frightened and immensely upset. "Joslyn," I ask as I start to make the call, "did you get hurt at all? Did you get hit by his..." I make a gesture above my head pantomiming his antlers. "If he hit you, I promise it was an accident."

"No," Joslyn replies, wiping more tears and snot from her face. "No, he didn't hurt me. I really didn't mean to scare him."

"You did nothing wrong, dear," I reply with as much sincerity as I can convey, just as Abby answers her phone. I excuse myself and speak to my wife. "Hey. We had a bit of an incident here at the Harpers. ... It's Andy. I don't know what happened, but..." I sigh. "His antlers came back again."

Andy

I can't believe it happened again. And in front of Joslyn. How could I let this happen? How could I not control this? I'm such an idiot. I lost my temper. Now she probably thinks I hate her. But I don't hate her. I swear! Will she ever want to talk to me again? Will she let me apologize? Will she let me explain what happened? Will she even understand? Or is it...hopeless?

I run into woods just outside the Harpers' neighborhood. I don't stop running. I run past all the fences and backyards. I run until it hurts, and I just kept running. I can feel my face get hit by sticks and branches, and I feel my antlers hit branches above my head. But I can't stop running. My legs carry me through the woods, over all the rocks and divots, past all the other houses and yards, and by some miracle, they bring me to my own backyard.

Our backyard is very long, and I'm still far from the house. I look around but don't see anyone. I catch my breath and head over to my favorite tree in the back corner. My parents know my favorite tree very well. They had to cut off all the lower branches so I wouldn't climb it when I got angry as a little kid. Instead, they set up a bench and a hammock chair for me, so I could have a place outside to sit and chill or draw.

I plop down on the bench and put my head in my hands, ready to burst into tears. I'm relieved that I made it to my own yard, but it doesn't make me feel better for long.

I can't believe I just ran out of Joslyn's house like that. I must have scared her real bad. I hope I didn't hurt her. Did I hurt her? I ran out so fast I didn't check. The thought of hurting her makes me cry harder. If I hurt her, everyone will surely be furious with me. I'll be grounded for life. And I'll deserve it. I thought I had fixed myself so this wouldn't happen again. But watching that interview with Mom, talking about how much those wings hurt her back and how those people didn't help her, just made me so angry and upset. And Joslyn saw me angry. And she saw me angry at her. Was I angry at her?

"Andy?"

I look up through the blur of my tears. "Mom?"

"Are you okay, buddy?" Mom asks gently.

I wipe my eyes to clear my vision. Mom is standing in front of me, using her cane. She walked all the way out here to check on me while her back still hurts?

"I'm so sorry, Mom," I say, crying. "I scared her, and I didn't mean to. And I didn't know how much you got hurt. And…"

"Shhh," Mom says. She sits down on the bench next to me and starts to stroke the back of my head to comfort me. "It's all right. Dad told me everything, so just let it all out."

I cry some more until I can calm down enough to look up. Mom wipes the tears from my cheeks and gives me her loving smile. "So, Dad says you watched the interview I did on *The Late Show*," Mom says gently. "Do you want to talk about it? Do you have any questions? Anything in particular that bothers you?"

I do my best to calm myself and stop crying. "Did you get angry?" I ask. "When…when everyone didn't help you? Or when everyone was using you? Did you get angry?"

"Not really," she answers with a smile.

"Really?"

"Yeah, really," she assures me. "I wasn't angry, because I *wanted* to do it. I wanted to play the part. I will admit I was sad when people winning awards didn't thank me for being part of their project, but I was never angry. Mason was more angry than I was."

"He was?"

"Yep. We've talked about it a lot over the years. I think he was angry he couldn't do more to help. Same as your father. He told me he felt so helpless that day. I have to keep reminding your dad that just him being there was the best part of that day. Whenever I needed him, he was right there by my side. If your father wasn't there, I probably would have been angry."

I wipe my nose with my wrist and take a breath. "If you could go back and do the movie again, would you?"

"Probably," Mom answers, to my surprise.

"Why?" I ask, almost getting angry again.

"Did you not see the end of the interview?" she asks.

I shake my head. "I stopped at the part where you were talking about the scars on your back."

"Ah," she responds. "Well, the host asked me the same question, and he was a little surprised by that answer too. I do wish everyone else treated me differently, and I wish I had taken better care of myself so I didn't injure myself as badly, but the story of the movie itself was beautiful. I got to work with some of my best friends, and I was so in love during the filming, it made me love the part and love the movie even more. I mean, really, it's a love story about a fallen angel looking to find who she was and with whom she belonged, and I was living in a moment, planning to marry the person with whom I belonged. How lucky was I to have such an opportunity as an actress, right?"

For some reason, Mom's explanation makes me cry again. But this time I'm not sad. At least, I don't think I'm sad.

"I didn't mean to scare Joslyn," I confess. "She wanted to play a game and, instead, we watched that video, and it made me mad. She probably thinks I'm angry with her. I accused her of trying to

tell me she knew more about you than I did, and then...then..."
I break down again. Mom puts her arm around me. "I think I
scared her, and now I don't know if she ever wants to see me again.
I want to be friends with her so much. She's so nice and I scared
her, and..."

"Shhh." Mom maneuvers her head around my antlers to put
her chin on top of my head like she used to when I was little. She
holds me tight, rubbing my arm. "It's okay. Really, it's okay. The
fact that you're so concerned about her is so amazingly sweet. I'm
so proud of you." Mom's words make me cry even more. "I'm
sure she likes you for who you are. You went out of your way to
stand up for her. That makes you a superhero to her."

"But I scared her so much," I cry. "She saw me with antlers,
and I scared her."

"Shhh shhh," Mom continues to comfort me. "Did I ever tell
you the story about how your father and I met?"

I take a few breaths. Why is Mom bringing this up now? "He
won some contest to meet you, right?"

"Sort of," Mom says. "Your father was chosen from a group of
writers to work with a famous Muse and create a character specifically for that Muse. And, by chance, he was matched with me. I
was only nineteen at the time, and he was in his early twenties. We
met for the first time at a rehearsal space at the studio. Walter was
with me, as well as the contest promoters. We took some photos
and then we sat down and started to chat. I honestly didn't expect
to get to know your father, because I figured I was just there to
help inspire some up-and-coming writer. And I was happy to be
that for someone if it helped them. I didn't expect to feel like I
had so much in common with him. We liked the same movies, the

same foods, a lot of the same music. I was still skeptical, because I'd met people who pretended to like me but really just wanted to get close to someone famous. But your father was different.

"So, the contest was basically designed so that the writer would get to meet with their chosen Muse a few times and then go and develop some character with a backstory for the Muse to then embody and perform a short scene or monologue. After meeting with me three times for several hours each time, your father ended up forfeiting the contest because, according to him, he couldn't change me. Instead, he wrote me a love letter confessing that he couldn't develop a character that could be anything but who I naturally was. He was always the hopeless romantic.

"I think he figured that letter would be the last time he'd get to see me. It was beautiful and sad. I read it and cried because it was just so touching, but I also didn't want that to be the last time we got to meet. I got his address, and I wrote him a letter back. It wasn't as flowery as his, but I wanted to thank him for his letter and tell him that I hoped it wouldn't be the last one. I started getting love letters almost every day after that, for almost a month before we got to meet again and go on our first date."

"So, Dad liked you for you?" I say.

"Still does," Mom replies with a smile. "When a girl finds someone who genuinely likes them for just who they are, it's the best feeling in the world. If that's how you like Joslyn, maybe you can tell her."

"But how?" I ask.

Just then, we hear the back door close and see Dad walking out into the backyard toward us. He waves and looks tired. "Hey, bud," he calls out. "Figured you ran home through the woods. How're you feeling?"

"A little better," I say, taking another staggered breath. "I'm sorry I ran away again. Are you mad?"

"No, I'm not mad," Dad says, joining Mom and me at the tree and taking a seat in the hammock chair. "Joslyn was very upset when you ran off. She was so afraid it was all her fault."

"She was?" I feel myself getting ready to cry yet again.

"But it's all right," Dad quickly reassures me. "Mrs. Harper calmed her down while I did a quick inspection of the back room and kitchen with Mr. Harper to make sure you didn't accidentally break anything, and everything is fine. I assured them you were all right and that this has happened before. They are concerned about you, though, and they want to make sure you're alright."

"They are?" I ask, feeling a little better.

"They are," Dad assures me. "Which reminds me." He reaches into his shirt pocket and pulls out a slip of paper, handing it to me. "Congratulations," he says, "you've gotten your first phone number from a cute girl."

I open the piece of paper and see a phone number and a note underneath. It reads:

Please call me.
–Joslyn

I don't know why, but that note makes me smile.

"How about this," Mom offers. "Let's go back to the house,

clean up your face, change clothes, make sure you're not bleed-ing out..."

I laugh at that comment, thinking I must look like a real mess after running through the woods.

"...and do a little bit of meditation to get rid of the rest of your antlers. Then, you can give her a call. Sounds good?"

The "rest" of my antlers? I reached up to touch my head. The antlers are down to just nubs. I don't know how she does it, but Mom knows how to ungrow my antlers.

Joslyn

After Mr. Bennett leaves, Momma makes me take a shower, wash my face, and put on my pajamas, even though it's only 3:00 in the afternoon. Momma sits with me on the couch in our living room and we watch cartoons. Watching cartoons always makes me feel better, and I kinda like when Momma watches them with me. I especially like when she laughs at the same jokes as me. Daddy's in the kitchen cleaning up all the dishes from lunch. I feel a little better.

Before Andy and Mr. Bennett came over, Momma and I had a long talk about what to talk about and what not to talk about. She explained that, at her hospital, they had really famous people come in sometimes, and it's her job to make sure all visitors and patients feel the same when they're there and that who they are, or how famous they are, isn't talked about while they're being treated. I thought I would be okay because I was more excited to see Andy than anything. I was more worried about Daddy saying something that would embarrass us.

I'd put all my folders and binders with pictures of movies away and tried to clean up anything I thought would make Andy think I was thinking of his mom while he was here and make him uncomfortable. In the end, I completely forgot about watching those videos on my tablet. And of course, that's what he found. I wish I had stopped him, but I let him watch the video instead. I didn't stop him, and he got upset. I made him feel so bad that he yelled at me. It was my fault he ran out of the house...

I feel myself getting sad again as I think about it more. I lean against Momma. She holds me tighter.

When Mr. Bennett asked if I was okay and told me he wasn't upset with me, it didn't help much. I knew he was trying to make me feel better, but I just didn't. Daddy walked him through the house, and Mr. Bennett seemed to inspect every ding in the walls and furniture from the sunroom to the door to see if it could have been something Andy bumped into and broke. Daddy was able to explain all the dents or dings Mr. Bennett found, and none of them seemed to have been caused by Andy running through the house with his antlers. I thought it was weird Mr. Bennett wanted to do that, but Momma explained afterward that that was so he could feel better before he left. It was his way of making sure we were all alright.

Before Mr. Bennett left, he made sure Daddy had his home and his cell phone numbers and made Daddy promise to call him if he found anything broken or damaged that could have been Andy's fault. Daddy then suggested I write down our home number to give to Andy, in case he wanted to call me later and talk.

"But," I said, "what if he doesn't want to call me?"

"Well, write him a note and ask him anyway," Daddy suggested.

Mr. Bennett took my number and note, thanked us again for lunch, then drove home. That's when Momma sent me to take a shower.

I try to focus on the cartoons, but I keep thinking about talking to Andy again. What if he did call? What would I say to him? What would he say to me? I imagine he'd just want to yell at me again, because he thought I made him watch that video. I would try to explain it was an accident, but he wouldn't listen, and he would just say to me, "I never want to talk to you again!" I can't change the thought in my head, and it just makes me more sad.

And whether or not he calls, I still have to see Andy at school. I will have to sit on the other side of the art classroom now, that's for sure. I'll have to make sure I don't look at him. He probably won't want to look at me. I'll have to pick the seat closest to the door, so I can get out fast when class is over. And if Mr. Castro wants to talk to me, I will tell him that I'm in a hurry and I'll see him after school. I can do that. I think I can do that.

It might be hard at first, but I'll get used to it. It'll be like my last school. And if I just keep bringing my books with me and reading during lunch, I won't have to see Andy if he has to come into the cafeteria to buy lunch or something. And I hardly see him walking in the halls or outside the school building when school lets out. If I do see him, I'll just look away quickly or look at the ground. I can do that. I think I can do that.

I can do that, but I don't *want* to do that.

I don't want to not talk to Andy again or not look at him or not sit next to him in class. I actually do want him to call. I want to talk to him. I want to make sure he's okay. I really want us to be friends! He's the only person my age who says they don't care what I look like or, even more, doesn't think others should care what I look like. He doesn't tell me I should wear more makeup or just cover my face with a bag like the kids at my last school. He doesn't encourage people to laugh like those boys in elementary school did. He actually told people to stop laughing. No one ever did that for me.

I want to get to know him better. I want to see more of his drawings. I want to know what books he likes, what music he likes, what video games he plays. I want to know what movies he likes, what shows he watches, where he likes to hang out when he's not at school. I want to show him my book collection, show him my favorite spots to explore or ride my bike. I want to play games on my tablets with him. I want another chance.

I want him to call so badly!

"Hello?"

I'm so distracted by my own thoughts, I don't hear the phone ring before Momma answers it.

"Oh, hi, baby," Momma says to the person on the phone. "We were so worried about you. How're you feeling? Did you make it home safe? ... Oh, don't worry about it, baby. We're all fine here. ... Let me ask her." Momma puts her hand on the receiver and turns to me. She says to me quietly, "It's Andy. Would you like to talk to him?"

I can feel my throat start to hurt and tears well up in my eyes as I nod my head yes. I very much want to talk to him. Momma hands me the phone, caresses my cheek gently, giving me a proud smile, then gets up from the couch to give me some privacy in the living room.

I put the phone to my ear and start to speak, hoping I don't sound like I'm going to cry. "Hello?"

"Hey, Joslyn," Andy says softly. He sounds sad. "I...um...I wanted to make sure you were okay. I'm sorry I scared you, and I'm really sorry I yelled at you. That was really stupid of me, and I'm sorry."

"It's okay," I say, barely getting the words out. "I'm really sorry too. I didn't mean to make you watch that video."

"What?" he replies, a little surprised. "What do you mean? You didn't make me watch that video. I should've just closed it and played the game with you like you wanted. I..." He makes a heavy sigh. "Thing is, I knew if I watched that I would probably get mad, but I did it anyway and, well, not only did I get stupid mad, I...I hurt you."

"You didn't hurt me!" I insist. "I'm fine. Really! I—"

"I mean I hurt your feelings," Andy continues. "See, ever since elementary school, kids were either scared of me or wanted to be friends with a really famous person's kid, even though I don't think my mom is really all that famous anymore. Then I would get teased by other kids, who said they knew more famous people than my mom. It really got bad for a while, but I kept it all inside. Then, the worst thing that happened was one of these kids who was bullying me...it turned out his dad was trying to steal something my dad had written and claim it as his own. When I heard that I...I blew up in front of everyone. All that anger made me grow antlers from the top of my head like you saw, but way bigger. I...I broke the ceiling, I hit my dad in the face with them. It got real bad. Mom had to come home early from a business trip and got there just in time to calm me down."

I don't say anything and just keep listening.

"After that, kids treated me differently. No one wanted to talk to me. Everyone was either afraid of me or thought I was weird. They didn't care to meet someone famous anymore either, because Mom had to meet them all to help apologize for what I did and make things right. Even though I didn't have antlers, I felt like everyone looked at me like I still did." Andy stops talking for a second, and I think I hear him sniffle. When he starts again, he sounds like he's crying. "I promised myself I'd never get that mad ever again, and I wouldn't let anyone make me feel like I was weird or different or a freak. And when those kids started saying stuff to you, I couldn't stand it. Because I know how it feels, and it's the worst." He stops again, sniffling a bit more. When he speaks again, I can tell he was definitely crying. "I'm really sorry I didn't stop myself from getting mad and scaring you and hurting your feelings. I don't know if you'll forgive me, but—"

"Yes!" I say, probably too fast. "Of course, I forgive you! You're right, it's bad when people look at you weird, but it's worse when you find out someone you love got hurt or wronged. It's normal to get mad about that stuff. I was afraid, but I was afraid I made you mad at me, and I didn't want you to be mad at me because I want us to be friends!"

There's a pause and another loud sniff. Then I hear what sounds like laughing. Is Andy laughing at me? Oh God, what did I do?!

"I want to be friends too," Andy says, sounding much happier. "I really want to be friends. I think you're awesome, and I want to hang out more. I mean, if you want to."

"Yes!" I say again. I feel myself getting happier. "Want to come over tomorrow? We'll be home from church after twelve."

"Um, sure," Andy replies happily. "Actually, that would be awesome. I can give you your invitation in person then."

"What invitation?" I ask.

"Mom wants me to invite you to come with us to the *Grace Falls* rerelease premiere this Friday," Andy says. "It's gonna be in one of those fancy theaters in the city. They're going to show the movie, and then Mom and some of the cast are going to answer some questions or something. She thought you might like to see that. Would you wanna go to that with me? I mean, with us?"

I'm in shock. I can't answer. I don't know how to answer. Andy's asking me to go to see *Grace Falls* with him? I have no answer. Well, that's not true. I have an answer. It's a really big *yes*! But it's not coming out. How long have I been quiet? He's going to think I've hung up if I don't say something fast!

What I want to tell Andy is that I want to go more than any-thing. I want to tell him that I want to go because he asked me, not because it's my favorite movie or because I might get to meet his mom. I actually don't care about those things. I have to tell him yes! I have to tell him I want to go!

"Let me check with Momma," I say.

What was that?! What the heck kind of answer was that?!

But Andy simply replies, "No problem. You can let me know when I come over tomorrow. Does 1:30 work for you?"

"1:30 is perfect," I say with no more pain in my throat and no more tears in my eyes. I'm happy. I'm really, really happy. "I'll see you tomorrow."

5

The Girl Who Grew Wings

Andy

Joslyn and Mr. Harper arrive at the house. Mr. Harper rings the buzzer, and I press the button to open the gate to let their car into the driveway. I run to the porch to let Mom know they're driving up. Gramma is getting ready to do Mom's hair and makeup, but Mom insists she wants to meet Joslyn at the door when she arrives.

All week, Joslyn could not stop talking about how excited she was to go to the movie premiere with me. She didn't talk about it like she was going to be meeting a lot of famous people (which she might) but like she was looking forward to an adventure. Dad offered to pick her up after school with me and bring her to the house, but she wanted to get ready at her house first before coming over. So Dad arranged everything with Mr. Harper and let him know to bring her over at 2:00 on Friday.

Joslyn hung out with me all week in Mr. Castro's classroom while I finished up the poster for Mom. She really did know the movie very well, as she helped me make sure the shape of the wings was just right. I ended up leaving the poster in Mr. Castro's classroom as I didn't want it to get messed up with all the chaos in the house today and figured I'd give it to Mom on Monday after her busy weekend.

After school, Joslyn and I chatted online about funny things we saw on the internet, our favorite songs and videos, all her favorite books, and all my favorite video games. Even though we hung out every day in school, I was looking forward to getting home and chatting with her more. I can't believe how fast we've become friends, and even after I scared her. She says she wasn't scared of my antlers; she was scared I was mad at her. I talked to Mom about it more, and she says it's okay that I was mad, but that I can try and find different ways and times to be mad. And because I wasn't, and I'm still not, mad at Joslyn, that I actually like her is very good.

Mr. Harper's car pulls up the driveway, and he parks behind Gramma's colorful station wagon. I watch through the front window as Joslyn and her dad walk up the rest of the driveway to the front door. Joslyn is wearing a very pretty red dress and matching bow in her hair. Red looks nice on her. I call out to Mom just as they ring the doorbell.

Mom rushes up to the front door, wearing her favorite hoodie and baggy yoga pants. Her hair is all tied up, and she's not wearing her makeup yet. She doesn't look like a movie star or anything. She just looks like Mom. I think that's what she wants too. I'm wearing a nice shirt and slacks. (I want to look a little nice. I think Mom wants that too.)

I open the door and greet Joslyn and Mr. Harper and let them in. Before Joslyn can take two steps, she is face to face with Mom, both wearing the biggest happiest smiles I've ever seen. Joslyn looks like she's going to cry as Mom opens her arms and gives her a big hug. Dad meets us in the foyer as well and shakes Mr. Harper's hand. We lead everyone into the house. Mom is talking to Joslyn and giving her a tour of the downstairs of our house and bringing her out to the porch where Gramma is setting up to do her hair and makeup. Mom introduces Joslyn to Gramma, then finally introduces herself to Mr. Harper, who doesn't seem upset that it took Mom so long to introduce herself. (Dad explains to me later that he was probably happier to see his daughter so happy than he was anxious to meet my mom.)

Gramma takes Joslyn's face in her hands and moves her head around as if to examine it. I suddenly feel super embarrassed. I should've warned Joslyn my gramma is weird. But Joslyn is laughing. I think she's enjoying it.

"Young lady," Gramma says, "your hair is absolutely amazing. Tell whoever did this that I want to take lessons from them."

"I did my hair," Joslyn says, still laughing. I like Joslyn's laugh.

Gramma lets go of her face. "Oh!" Gramma exclaims. "Then let me know when your next appointment is!"

Gramma then introduces herself to Mr. Harper, and for the first time, I think Mr. Harper is actually speechless. He's stuttering as he shakes her hand. "I have to tell you," Mr. Harper says, "when my wife and I were first dating, we found out we both of us loved your show *The Chameleon*. We practically bonded over our love for your show."

"That. Is. So. Touching," Gramma replies so sweetly. "You tell your wife she has good taste in men."

"I certainly will." Mr. Harper chuckles nervously.

Gramma then shoos us out so she can finish doing Mom's hair and makeup. Dad entertains Mr. Harper, and I go upstairs to finish getting dressed. I put on my favorite suit, which I laid out last night. But I change my tie from the green one I picked to one with red in it. I want to find something that matches Joslyn's dress. I also take out one of my fancy gray caps to wear, since I still have the patches on my head from the antlers last weekend. I had been hiding them under a beanie all week, and they still haven't filled in.

I come down the stairs and find Joslyn sitting at the breakfast bar in my normal seat as our dads are chatting in the kitchen. Joslyn sees me coming down the stairs and smiles. I think she likes what I'm wearing. I smile too.

"Look at this dapper man," Mr. Harper says, looking impressed. "I approve of a man who knows how to dress for a date with my daughter."

"Daddy!" Joslyn exclaims.

Dad explains the schedule for the evening, as there is a lot going on, and Mom and Dad are technically working tonight, so Gramma is going to be Joslyn's and my chaperone. There's a car coming to pick my parents up at 3:30, and Gramma is going to drive us separately. The theater has a mezzanine, and we're going to sit in the front row there to watch the movie, while Mom and Dad sit on the main floor with the rest of the cast. After the movie, there's going to be a short break, then they're going to hold a Q&A session with Mom and other cast members of the movie. After that, Gramma's going to bring Joslyn home. (I asked Mom and Dad earlier in the week if Joslyn could stay the night, but they didn't think her parents would be comfortable with that.)

After Dad finishes explaining the plan, Mr. Harper turns to me. "I'm counting on you to make sure she has a good time," he says to me sternly.

"Yes, sir," I respond proudly. "No crying, unless it's at the movie. Promise." I look at my dad. He gives me a thumbs up and a wink.

* * *

As we drive up to the theater, we see a bunch of press and people gathered outside along a red carpet. It seems crowded and busy, nothing like you see on TV. Joslyn and I are sitting in the back seat. Joslyn is on the side with the theater. She's staring out the window so close I wonder if her nose is pressed up against it. The thought makes me smile and almost laugh.

Gramma drives into a designated parking garage, and we follow her up and into a side entrance to the theater. We find the special VIP desk and meet a Miss Seitz, who says she is "entrusted" to show us around before taking us to our seats. Joslyn beams at the idea of going on a tour. She's so, so happy.

We walk through the bottom floor and see all the VIP reserved seats in the theater. Miss Seitz then lets us on the stage where they're going to have the Q&A. Joslyn sits in Mom's chair, and I sit in Uncle Mason's chair.

I turn to Joslyn. "Tell us, Miss Andrews," I say, "what was it like making this awesome movie?"

"It was a dream come true," she says in a silly, actress-like voice. She's smiling at me big now. I think I might be blushing, because my face feels hot.

We then meet the camera operators who're going to be filming the Q&A and watch them test their equipment. After that, we go to the green room, where they've laid out snacks for everyone. We aren't allowed to take any. Gramma says they aren't that great anyway. Miss Seitz laughs nervously.

Finally, we go to our seats in the front row mezzanine for the movie. I sit between Joslyn and Gramma. The seats are amazing. We're not quite center, but we have a perfect view of the screen. Joslyn is literally bouncing with excitement. I can tell she wants to say a lot but is trying to contain herself. I'm so happy she's here with me. I don't know if I would have wanted to come if she had turned down the invitation.

People start to come into the theater and fill the seats. Gramma points out some of the more recognizable people or people she's known for a long time. She says a lot of them are probably here because they got special invitations from the producers, or their agents pulled strings to get them invites. But Gramma is sure to name everyone she thinks is especially there to support Mom. Joslyn keeps bouncing and smiling and pointing but doesn't say anything.

We continue watching as people file in. The theater gets louder and louder. Finally, I see Dad walk in with Uncle Thomas. They're both wearing very nice tuxedos. I wonder if I should've worn a tux now. They go to their seats in the fifth row. Dad turns around and points out to Uncle Thomas where we're sitting. I stand up from my seat and wave down to them. I then turn to Joslyn and hold out my hand to help her up. She takes my hand and stands up next to me and waves down at my dad. I lean over and whisper to Joslyn that Uncle Thomas is Uncle Mason's husband. Joslyn just smiles and waves more. Uncle Thomas blows me a kiss. Joslyn giggles, and I rub the back of my neck. He didn't have to do that, did he? Dad gives him a pat on the back, and they both take a seat.

Joslyn and I start to sit down, when I realize we've been holding hands the whole time. I look at her a little embarrassed and gently let go. She just keeps smiling.

Not long after, the lights go down and the stage lights up. Then, Charles Russell, who is a famous actor I recognize, comes onto the stage and introduces himself as the host and moderator for the evening.

Joslyn bounces in her seat more and puts her hand on my knee. I feel my cheeks get hot again, but I don't do anything to tell her to take her hand away.

Charles introduces several people from the cast, who all walk on the stage. As everyone is introduced, Joslyn applauds happily. She points at the stage and looks at me like she wants to say, "Do you see who that is?" I smile and clap with her.

"And finally," Charles says, "it is my absolute honor and pleasure to introduce the stars of *Grace Falls*, Abby Andrews and Mason Drake." The theater fills with cheers and applause. Everyone jumps to their feet to clap for Mom and Uncle Mason. Mom is holding onto Uncle Mason's arm as they walk up onto the stage together. Uncle Mason is wearing a very fancy black suit and tie, and Mom's wearing a very pretty white dress with flowers and a nice flowy scarf draped over her back.

"She looks like she has wings," Joslyn says to me as her whole arms seem to clap for Mom.

She's right, I think. Mom's dress does look like she kinda has wings.

Mom dabs her eyes with a handkerchief, mouthing "Thank you" to everyone. I feel myself want to cry, and I reach up to wipe my eyes. Joslyn must've seen, because she reaches to take my hand again. She gives it a little squeeze and gives me a big smile. That makes me feel better.

Mom makes her way down the line of cast members and gives them kisses and hugs. Everyone looks so happy to see her, even Christophe Holtz, the actor who played the scary preacher. I know he's really a nice person in real life, but it's still weird to see him hug Mom and kiss her cheek. Finally, Mom gives Charles a kiss and hug. Charles looks like he's going to cry now. I wonder if he's also a big fan of Mom's.

Charles then explains to the audience that everyone will be back on stage for a discussion panel afterward. "But now, let's enjoy the fully remastered, fully unmatched classic *Grace Falls*."

The audience applauds again, and the lights in the theater go down as we all sit down again.

As the opening credits and shots of mountains fill the huge screen, I remember the first time Mom let me watch this movie. It actually wasn't all that long ago. She said I had to be over ten years old to see it, because there were parts in it she didn't want me to see until I was older. I never asked her which parts those were.

I had always assumed it was the part with the wings, since that might have been too scary for me when I was little.

The shots go from the mountains to the town and the people walking around and...wait a minute, was that customer exiting the general store Dad? I'd have to ask him after the movie.

The movie plays on, and the scene where Grant first finds Celeste injured and abandoned in the woods comes up. Just then, I feel Joslyn take my hand again and hold it tight. I glance over at her. A few tears fall down her cheek. I don't take my hand away. I don't hold it too tight, so if she decides to take it away, she can.

Then the scene where Grant's father, the town's "fire and brimstone" preacher, scolds his son for caring about the "outsider" Celeste more than his betrothed comes up. I feel Joslyn squeeze my hand. I squeeze her hand a little too. I think she likes it, because she holds my hand a little tighter than before.

Finally, the movie's most famous scene is coming up. Celeste is chased out of the town, and Grant runs after her. He finds her at the mountain edge, just outside town, as the sky opens and the rain falls harder over both of them. Celeste looks like she wants to jump when Grant shows up and begs for her to stay with him. When he confesses his love, Joslyn and I hold each other's hand tighter.

"Stay back!"

I didn't tell Joslyn that I was scared to watch this scene again after learning about Mom's injuries. I couldn't decide if I was going to try and watch it, or if I was going to look away. I glance again over at Joslyn and notice, this time, she's looking at me. She's smiling, and she squeezes my hand, like she's telling me we're in this together.

As Celeste's wings grow greater and greater, I remember what Mom said about how she was feeling filming the movie. How she was in love, like Celeste was falling in love. Celeste was discovering who she really was, and she had to admit it to the person she loved if she was going to be happy. Wait...that's it! I get it now! This scene isn't about hurting; it's about finally *not* hurting. Celeste was holding in everything she was inside, and as she grows her wings, she lets it all out.

Celeste releases her wings and then stands up strong and proud. And Grant doesn't run away. He stays and he loves her just as she is.

As I think about it, I start to cry.

I'm so glad Joslyn's holding my hand right now.

* * *

The standing ovation after the movie keeps going and going, but Joslyn and I stand for all of it. After everyone settles again, Charles Russell comes back on the stage and announces that there will be a twenty-minute intermission before the Q&A panel. Gramma offers to get us each a soda from the bar so we can stay in our seats. She then leaves me and Joslyn alone.

"So," I say, "what did you think seeing the movie on the big screen like this?"

"This was the most amazing experience ever," she says joyfully. "I don't know how to thank you enough for asking me to come."

"You can thank my mom," I say, rubbing the back of my neck. "I feel weird taking the credit for this. It was really her idea for me to ask you."

"But you were still the one to ask me," Joslyn says.

Oh gosh. I think I'm blushing again.

"Um," Joslyn continues hesitantly, "I have a question about your mom if it's okay to ask."

"Please," I say. "Please ask your question. I don't mind."

"Um," Joslyn starts to say, still hesitant, "your mom still helps teach people how to be a Muse, right?"

"Sometimes," I answer. "She helps actors and actresses improve their techniques, mostly when she's asked. Why?"

"Um," Joslyn continues, "do you think she could teach me a little?"

"You...want to be a Muse?" I ask a little surprised.

"I..." she says, "I'm wondering if she could teach me how to grow wings of my own." She looks up at me and gets immediately defensive. "I don't mean really big ones. I just want to see if I can."

"But, why wings?" I ask.

"Because I think wings made her look so beautiful," she answers. "I never thought the wings looked scary or ugly. I think they're beautiful. And I want to look beautiful like her too. Also..." Joslyn trails off and looks at her lap.

"What?" I ask concerned.

"I read somewhere that Muses can also change their skin color, make it a little darker or lighter than their natural color if they really wanted to. If it's true, I'm wondering if maybe she could help me with that too. I know that will make me look beautiful too. Do you think she could teach me?"

Oh, Joslyn. I have to tell her the truth. I take both of her hands and I look her in the eyes. "You can ask my mom all that stuff, but since you're asking me, I'm going to tell you, you don't need all that. I think you're already beautiful."

Joslyn blushes and smiles. She's so pretty when she smiles.

"And if anyone tells you otherwise, you let me know. I'll give 'em the antlers."

Joslyn laughs loud enough that people look at us, but I don't care. I made her laugh and that makes me happy.

Joslyn

The weekend after we went to see *Grace Falls*, Andy's parents invite me and my parents over to their house for a movie night party in their backyard. They didn't say what movie was going to play, except it's not going to be *Grace Falls*. "Mom was tired of watching it after the fourth time last weekend," Andy explained when he gave me the invite.

Momma was able to switch shifts at the hospital so she could come too. And she insisted that we bring something to contribute to the party. Miss Andrews said she heard great things about Momma's chicken, if she wanted to bring that, but not to feel obligated. Little does Miss Andrews know that nothing makes Momma happier than to make her chicken for others.

I also told Momma that I didn't want to wear makeup to the party. I told her what Andy said when I asked if his mom could teach me to change my skin color, that he thought I was already pretty and didn't need to change anything, and that I wanted to try and go out without wearing makeup for once. That made Momma very happy too.

We arrive at Andy's house Saturday afternoon. Andy's grandmother's car is in the driveway too. Daddy turns to me and gives me a wink. When Momma asks what that was about, we just say, "Nothing."

We go to the door, and I ring the doorbell, and Andy answers. I didn't think about it until that second, that this will actually be the first time Andy sees me without makeup. I get a little nervous. What's he going to say? How's he going to react?

Andy sees me at the door and just smiles. It's his usual smile too. Like there's nothing different or weird or wrong. I like Andy's smile. It makes me happy.

He lets us into the house and shows us to his backyard, which is huge! They set up a big projection screen in the middle of the lawn and lots of different chairs and seats all over the yard facing the screen. Andy points out a pair of beanbag chairs close to the screen that he saved for us. Andy's dad is setting up the projector on a table in the middle of all the seats. Mr. Bennett stops and comes over to shake Daddy's hand. He then reaches out to Momma to shake her hand. She takes it and pulls him into a hug. I roll my eyes. I don't always like it when Momma hugs people like that, but Mr. Bennett doesn't seem offended.

Just then, Miss Andrews and Miss Dee Dee come out to the backyard, carrying more fun chairs. When we see them, I immediately look at Momma. This is the first time she's going to meet them.

Momma's mouth opens wide, and she puts her hands on her chest. She's completely surprised. She looks at all of us like we set up this surprise just for her.

Mr. Bennett guides her over and introduces her to Andy's mom and gramma. Momma takes Miss Dee Dee's hands in hers, and we watch her confessing just how huge a fan she is of hers and how much her show, *The Chameleon*, meant to her growing up. Miss Dee Dee listens to every word and keeps holding Momma's hands tightly. Andy's gramma is so awesome.

Andy shows me around his huge yard and takes me to the tree in the back corner. He says this is the spot he hangs out the most. His parents set up a bench and a hammock chair for him so he can either hang out by himself or with friends. This is so great! Andy's showing me one of the places he likes to hang out!

Daddy helps Mr. Bennett connect the projector to his tablet in order to play the movie. I can hear Daddy explain things about their internet settings and other suggestions to improve their internet connection around their house. Miss Andrews and Miss Dee Dee sit and chat with Momma. I remembered to bring my tablets, and Andy and I sit down on the bench in his hangout spot and play games.

"Remind me to show you my video games before you leave," Andy says. "I don't know if you have a game system, but if you do, you're welcome to borrow anything I have."

Yes! Andy's going to show me what video games he likes to play!

After a little while, we hear the doorbell ring. More guests are coming. Miss Andrews answers the door, and we hear loud and happy greetings. A moment later, Miss Andrews comes to the backyard with Mason and Thomas Drake. Andy takes my hand and, with a lot of excitement, introduces me to them.

"Uncle Mason, Uncle Thomas, this is my friend Joslyn," he says. "She's the friend I brought to the premiere last week."

"Oh, this was your date for the movie!" Mr. Thomas exclaims enthusiastically, reaching out his hand to me.

I take his hand, expecting to shake it, but instead he kisses my wrist.

"Uncle Thomas," Andy grumbles, clearly embarrassed. Andy's response makes me giggle. He gets embarrassed at his family just like me.

After Mr. Thomas lets my hand go, Mr. Mason shakes my hand normally. "A pleasure to meet you," he says. "Any friend of Andy's is our friend too. What did you think of the whole show last weekend? You enjoy the movie?"

"Yes!" I say enthusiastically. "That was so amazing. I...I can't describe how amazing it was. I really liked the panel afterward and hearing you all talk about your experience making the movie."

The doorbell rings and more people arrive. Mr. Walter arrives along with Miss Martha and Miss Fortune from his office. I recognize Walter Saint James from the panel after the movie. He was Miss Andrews's Creator for many years. Andy gives him a big hug and introduces me to him too. Miss Martha and Miss Fortune apparently work with Mr. Walter at Reimagine Productions and know Mr. Bennett really well. Mrs. Reynolds arrives next, with her husband and little baby boy. Miss Andrews is super happy to see them when they arrive and is super excited to see Mrs. Reynolds's baby. Andy explains that Mrs. Reynolds was his mom's personal assistant, but she's on a break because she had her baby. That's why his dad has been acting as his mom's assistant lately.

Finally, to our surprise, Mr. Castro and his wife arrive at the party. Apparently, Andy didn't know his mom had invited Mr. Castro to their movie night. Andy's super happy to see his favorite teacher and introduces Mr. and Mrs. Castro to everyone. It makes me happy to see Andy so proud of his family. Mrs. Castro's a little starstruck meeting Andy's mom and Mr. Mason, but Mr. Castro helps keep her calm. Miss Andrews thanks Mr. Castro for being so supportive of Andy and also for helping him with the poster Andy made for her.

I almost forget this will also be the first time Mr. Castro will see me without my makeup. I go up to say hi, and when Mr. Castro sees me, he gave me the biggest smile.

"I hope you don't mind me saying," he says, when no one can hear, "but I think I prefer the no makeup look on you. But that's just me." He gives me his signature wink, which is different from Mr. Bennett's.

Just then, Andy remembers something, and he runs around the side of the house. Miss Dee Dee invites everyone to get something to eat and drink before the movie starts. They have a spread of all kinds of snacks, including Momma's chicken and Miss Andrews's favorite potato salad. I make myself a plate and sit in one of the beanbag chairs. There's a paper bag sitting next to Andy's seat.

"That's for you," he says, "but don't open it until I get there."

"Okay," I reply.

I take my seat and look up at the screen to see what movie we're watching. It's the newest Spider-Man movie.

Andy sits down in his chair and looks up at the screen too. "Yes!" he exclaims. "I love this movie!"

Oh my gosh! Something else Andy likes!

"Oh," he then says, looking over, "you can open your present now."

"My present?" I ask.

Andy gestures to the bag next to my chair. I pick it up and look inside. "Ooo! A plant with red flowers!"

"It's an angel wing begonia plant," Andy says. "I found it when Dad and I went shopping today. The color reminded me of your dress last week. Plus, now you can grow wings. Just like you wanted. Do you like it?"

"I love it," I say. "This makes me so happy. Thank you so much, Andy."

Three

The Boy Who Grew Up

1

The Boy Who Had a Headache

Andy

I wait outside the side entrance for Joslyn to come out so we can walk to our coffee shop like we've done every Friday since we started high school. We just finished our first week back after winter break, and the air's still cold and dry. I'm really looking forward to that coffee.

I'm also looking forward to working on our story again. We had been working on this comic book idea since summer, and our family trip up to Washington State for Christmas gave me some great ideas for settings for the next part. Now I'm standing here, anxious to show her my sketches and get her opinion. Well, that and a hot coffee.

Joslyn finally emerges, talking with a couple girls from her history class. "Hey Andy!" she calls out with a wave. "Sorry for taking so long. Give me one more sec?"

"Sure," I say with a smile. I watch as Joslyn turns and appears to help one of the girls pull something up on her phone, possibly for an assignment they have over the weekend. She's in so many study groups, I wouldn't be surprised. Jos says her goodbyes and we're off to coffee. Finally!

"So," she starts. "How was your first week?"

"Eh," I reply. "New teachers. New textbooks. Whatever. You like your classes?"

"For the most part, yeah," she says casually but positively. "I finally have a history class with Mr. Dunbar, which I love! He doesn't take anything from anyone. Not those smartass dudes that sit in the other's seats and pretend to be a different student. Not from those girls that come in late with wet hair because they can't show up for school on time. It's gonna be glorious to watch him work. Speaking of watching teachers work, I meant to ask you earlier. I thought you signed up for the creative writing class with me. Didn't you want to watch your dad teach his first ever high school class?"

"Yeah, I kinda chickened out," I confess, rubbing the back of my neck. "I didn't want to be judged hard by the class or the teacher for being the teacher's son. He's treating you right, though? I don't need to talk to him for you? I'll beat him up if you need me to."

Joslyn laughs and hits my arm with the back of her hand. I pretend it hurts and she laughs a little more.

"Your dad's fine. Leave him alone."

"Well, you let me know if you need me to get your grade changed or something. 'Cause I'll do it."

"You know what you could do is beat up those jerks who teased you at lunch the other day," Joslyn offers sympathetically.

"Eh, they're harmless," I say dismissively. "I'll just ignore them."

We approach the intersection across from Café Cocoa, and we fall into awkward silence. I can't tell why it's awkward; it's just something in the air. Or in the silence.

"Um," Joslyn starts to say. I know when she starts anything with "um," it's going to be an uncomfortable question for one of us. "I was thinking about going to the spring dance this year."

"Oh?" I say. That wasn't what I was expecting.

"You think you'd want to go this year?" she asks.

"I don't know," I answer honestly. "Dances make me uncomfortable."

"Oh, okay," Joslyn says. I don't like the sound of that. She sounds disappointed.

"Did I say something wrong?" I ask.

"No. Forget it," she replies, trying to be dismissive. Dammit, I upset her. And just as I'm about to probe further, the light changes, and Jos immediately starts to cross the street. I nearly trip trying to catch up with her. I wish she'd just tell me when I'm about to upset her. It'd be easier than trying to read her mind. God knows I'll never be able to do that.

We enter the coffee shop and get into the short line to order our drinks.

"Oh," Joslyn says, nudging my arm and sounding less upset, "there's a guy in your dad's class that I think is new to the school, but your dad seemed to know him."

"Really?" I ask. "What's the guy's name?"

Rick

Abby's sitting at the dining room table staring at her laptop when I come home. I just finished my first week as a solo teacher of high school creative writing and am thoroughly drained. Only twenty-one more weeks to go, I think to myself with bleeding sarcasm.

"Welcome home!" Abby greets me, getting up to give me a kiss and help me with my bags.

She's really trying to lean into the stay-at-home-wife-and-mother role she took on last fall. I'm still on the fence as to whether or not I like this new role of hers, but regardless, I'm immensely proud of her for her dedication. She seems happier in many ways. Lost in others, though. We'll see how it goes.

"How was your day?"

"I'm learning pretty quickly that I loathe faculty meetings," I reply, taking off my shoes and necktie. "Thankfully, I got confirmation that I do not need to wear one of these damn ties ever again. What did you do today?"

"I washed our bedsheets and remade our bed," she starts, counting the tasks on her hand. "I spent lunch looking up recipes for ground turkey and mushrooms, stopping myself from checking email about 150 times, and..." She pauses to think, tilting her head ever so slightly as she focuses on a mystery point beyond the room that has been feeding her the answers. "I'm sure there had to be something else, but I can't think of it."

"I hope *rest* was one of those things," I say, taking a water bottle from the fridge. Abby sighs. "Honey, if you're going to take time off from working all the time, stop trying to find work."

Abby sighs harder and walks back into the dining room. Great, now she's upset. Well, at least I have an idea why.

I follow her into the dining room and sit in the chair across from her. She's buried herself in her laptop again. "Abby," I start gently, "I know it's been hard to slow down and decompress. You've been working for practically forty years straight. The fact that you're actually trying is amazing. But slowing down doesn't mean you have to stop everything. Maybe we just need to find a new outlet for some of this energy. Have you thought about doing something for yourself?"

"Well," she says meekly, "there was something."

"What is it?"

"What do you think about me trying to write...something?"

"Perfect!" I exclaim. And I mean it too. "I don't need to hear anything else. Write something. Whatever you want."

"That's the thing," she continues. "I've actually never written anything. I mean nothing creative or narrative."

"Who said it has to be narrative?" I ask. "Write what you want. Whatever's in your head. Poetry. Editorial. Informational. As you put it, something!"

"Would you help me?" she asks with some trepidation.

"I'll grade your work with my students' work," I offer cheekily.

She sticks her tongue out at me but can't hide her grin as she does it. God, my wife is gorgeous.

"I'm actually trying to figure out a way for students to submit their work to me anonymously, anyway, so I don't unintentionally impose biases on the students I know. You know Joslyn's in my class, right?"

"She told me she signed up for it. Did Andy tell you why he changed his mind on taking it?"

"I figured he got cold feet about being in a creative writing class with his dad and his girlfriend."

"What did I tell you about calling Andy and Joslyn boyfriend and girlfriend?"

It's true, Abby really dislikes when I say that, but to my credit I never call them by those titles in front of them. But I'm not the only one calling them a couple. David, Joslyn's dad, is constantly referring to them as "the cute couple." And like my wife, Joslyn's mother scolds her husband for doing so. Like Abby, Monica would prefer our children figure out they're a couple for themselves.

Just then, Andy comes home, dropping his coat at the front door.

"Welcome home, son!" I call out from the dining room.

He doesn't answer. That's unusual.

"Everything alright?"

"Yeah," Andy calls out. "I'm going to bed."

That's even more unusual. Abby looks up from her laptop and shoots me a concerned expression. I put up my hand to let her know I'll check on him. She smiles and mouths the words "Thank you" to me.

I get up and walk to the foyer, catching Andy just as he's about to head up the stairs. "Bud," I say, "you okay?"

"I just got a headache," he replies. He's avoiding eye contact with me.

"Everything okay with you and Jos?" I ask, knowingly jumping to an assumption.

This makes Andy look at me. Now he looks furious. At me or something else?

"You...need to talk about it?" I ask, intentionally jumping to another assumption. "Something I did?"

Andy breaks eye contact again.

"If you don't talk about it, you're going to worry your mother, y'know."

That makes Andy bolt up the stairs. I hear the door to his room slam.

Dammit, I failed.

"Do you know what that was about?" Abby asks, walking into the foyer.

"I might have an idea," I say. "I wonder if Jos told him about the new student in her writing class."

Andy

Bruno!

Why the hell did it have to be Bruno?!

What the hell is he doing at my school?

And why is he in Dad's class? With Jos?

And why didn't Dad tell me?

I thought after he'd been taken out of my elementary school that would be the last time I'd have to see him. His parents had separated, and he moved with his mom out of town during their divorce. I thought I'd never have to see him again. But now...

What the hell?!

When Joslyn told me, I couldn't say anything. I'd never told her all the details of that day. I never gave her names. When she told me, my head started to ache. Then it began to pound. I was in so much pain I had to cut our coffee short and come home. I kept reaching for my head to make sure I wasn't growing antlers. Joslyn could tell I wasn't telling her everything. And if she wasn't already frustrated with me for telling her I didn't want to go to the dance, she probably would've given me another pass. Instead, I kept getting the "short answer" treatment. The "okays" and the "whatevers."

I plop face down in my bed, holding a pillow over the back of my head in some vain, and probably stupid, attempt to relieve the pain. All I could do was scream into my other pillow.

What the hell?!

Why did I drop out of Dad's class? I could've been there! But I didn't want to be there. I didn't want to be in a class with Bruno. Why would I want to be there?

My head is pounding, and now I'm thinking in circles.

Or is it Joslyn? Is this some stupid logic about protecting her? Why would she need protection? Why do I feel this intense need to protect her all of a sudden? Is it because I upset her?

I'm so confused. And now my head hurts even more.

Maybe I needed to go back to therapy.

I should probably text Jos, I think to myself. I bet she's worried.

But why would she be worried? I wonder. She's actually probably not worried. She's probably upset.

I just want to scream. I don't know what to do or who to talk to. I feel trapped. Gah! I'm so frustrated!

I know I have to let it out somehow. Before the antlers come back. Mom and Dad said I could always talk to them whenever I feel, y'know, antler-y. But Mom's been busy trying to be a stay-at-home mom, and, I dunno, I can't help but feel like part of this is Dad's fault. Like, why didn't he tell me Bruno was in his class? With Jos?

In my school? With me? Me and Jos?

Should I tell Jos about Bruno?

Ahhh! My head's pounding more and more as I keep thinking about Bruno. I turn over in my bed and hold my pillow tight around the back of my head and ears. I have to try and stop thinking about him. It's the only way to get rid of this headache. So, instead I try to think about Joslyn. About how I can make her, well, un-upset.

What did I do again to upset her? Maybe I should retrace my steps. We were crossing the street. No, it was before that. What were we talking about before that? Those jerks at lunch. No, after that. That's right. She asked me something. She asked me something about the spring dance. She was thinking about going and...

I sit up in my bed and cup my face in my hands. I am so stupid.

She was asking if I wanted to go to the spring dance...with her. That's why she was upset.

Dammit, I am so dense. I need to apologize for misinterpreting her question. I look over at my nightstand and pick up my phone. I pull up text chat with Joslyn, and—

Well, wait, if I'm going to apologize for that, maybe I should answer her actual question. The answer is obviously...

It's obviously...

What is the answer? I mean, if she needs someone to go with her to the spring dance, of course, I'll go. But who *needs* someone to go to a school dance with them? Neither of us drive or have a car. And she has her girlfriends from her history class now. But she wasn't asking me because she needed someone to go with.

I drop my head back and groan in more frustration. I'm a stupid idiot.

Joslyn was asking me out.

Dammit, I'm so dense. And stupid. And confused. And frustrated. And none of this is helping my worsening headache.

Gaaaah!

I hear a soft knock on the door.

"Andy?" It's Mom. "Andy, I'm opening the door. Is that alright?"

"Yeah, Mom," I say, tossing my phone back on my nightstand without texting Jos.

Mom gently opens the door and peeks her head in. "Honey, I heard you had a headache, so wanted to bring you some headache medicine and a glass of water. Here, I'll put them on your desk, okay?"

"Thanks, Mom," I say watching her from my seat on the bed.

Mom places a bottle of migraine medicine and a tall glass of water on a cleared patch of desk. "Also, I'm attempting to make turkey mushroom burgers for dinner," she says. "They'll probably end up tasting like crap, but I think it'll make you feel better if you eat something."

I kinda chuckle at that, which makes Mom smile.

"I'll text you when they're done, and you can let me know if you want me to bring some up for you, okay?"

"Okay," I reply. "Thanks, Mom."

Mom smiles and closes the door. My room is dark. I didn't

turn on any lights when I came in, and it has gotten dark outside. I get up out of my bed and take the pain meds and drink the whole glass of water. I then plop back down in my bed—face up this time—and turn on the lamp on my nightstand so I have some light. I grab my phone again and hold it above my head. I want to text Jos, but I need to figure out what to say.

I unlock my phone and see she's already texted me:

> *Hey! Just wanted to check on you and see how your head-ache is doing. Drink lots and get some good sleep.*
> *Don't make me worry :)*

I smile. She was worried, I was right. And I guess she wasn't so upset that she couldn't leave me a smile emoji. That makes me feel a little better. Not the headache, though. The drugs haven't kicked in yet.

I text back:

> *Thanks :) Will do. And I'm sorry I made you upset today while we were chatting. About going to the spring dance, can I get back to you later on that?*

I send the message.

Triple dots blink, then I get her text:

> *OK :)*

> *Your vacation pictures gave me a great idea about*

Athea's mountaintop battle. I'll write it up and send you a draft this weekend.

I write my reply:

Can't wait! I was thinking of trying a different artistic style for the mountain scenes as well. If I have time, I'll sketch them up and show you on Monday. I found some examples and added them to our Pinterest. Let me get the link.

Jos and I text back and forth for another half hour before I get a text from Mom letting me know dinner's ready. I tell Mom I'm feeling a little better, and I'll come down for dinner in a sec. I then text Jos that I need to go.

Quick triple dots blink, and I get her reply.

OK :)

Joslyn

"Alrighty. Before we wrap up today, it took me all weekend, but I think I figured out how I want everyone to submit your creative assignment," Mr. Bennett announces. He pulls out a costume top hat, shakes it a bit, reveals a bunch of paper, and places it back down on his desk.

The class chuckles at the sight.

"In this hat are slips of paper. On each paper is written a unique, and rather boring, email address and password. This will be your creative writing assignment mailbox for this class. Any creative writing assignments I give you, I want you to submit it to me using this email account. Let me stress, this is for your creative writing assignments. We'll be calling these 'By: Anonymous' assignments. Any other assignments, like your essays, editorials, reports...those will be turned in through the normal channels.

"Your mission—and you're required to accept it—" Only a few of us laugh at that one "—will be to not identify yourself by name or any other obvious clues on or in any of your creative writing assignments. If you do, you run the risk of being approached by me with a finger shake and harsher critiques for the rest of the semester. My hope is that we can all be critical of each other's writing by its content and not by the person behind the pen. I hope we can all do this.

"Your first assignment, however, will be to log into your account and send me an email simply saying, in no more than four words, 'Hi.'"

The class chuckles again.

"You will also need to go into this online spreadsheet, the link for which I will send everyone this evening, and fill in your name and the email address you drew from the hat. I'm going to ask one of my faculty colleagues to help me check that everyone filled it in and let me know who hasn't, so I can publicly shame you in front of your classmates."

Once again, the class laughs.

"You will have until Friday to log into your account, send me a message saying 'Hi,' and enter your information in the spreadsheet. It's basically a pass/fail assignment and I *will* be grading you. Responsibility, accountability, and deadlines are real-world attributes that I want you to take seriously. Any questions?"

No one raises their hand.

"Okay, I'm going to pass the hat around. Please only take one slip, and for the love of all things holy, don't read your email address out loud. I spent all weekend trying to think of a way to keep you all anonymous, so don't ruin my victory."

Mr. Bennett has a really good way of making our class relax. We all know he's being serious, but he also makes himself approachable. He really takes his craft seriously, and he's taking to teaching it passionately. I really get the feeling he wants everyone to succeed. How he grades us, however, has yet to be seen.

Everyone takes a slip of people with an email address. Mine's RBCW301.BA451@spjaca.com.

After he finishes distributing email addresses, Mr. Bennett closes out the class with a review of our homework. "Alright, what is everyone's assignment due Friday?"

The class says, in some jumble, that we all need to log into and register our new email address.

"And what's your assignment due tomorrow?"

Again, the class replies with "Read 'My Dying Garden.'"

"And write down some of your thoughts on it," Mr. Bennett concludes. "I don't care if it's some bullet points or an essay or a full-fledged thesis, but whatever you write, I will be collecting it, so make sure it's on paper and it does have your name on it. Any questions?"

No one has any questions.

"I'm holding you to that," he says. "Talk amongst yourself

until the bell. I'll be at my desk judging your conversations if you have any questions."

Again, the class laughs.

I start to put my books away and pull out my tablet to pick something to read at lunch. Andy had suggested a number of comics in the art style he was thinking of trying for the mountain scenes in our story, so I downloaded them last night. I happen to glance up and notice that new guy I had told Andy about—Bruno—get up and approach Mr. Bennett. Mr. Bennett appeared to know him well when he first came to class last week. When Bruno gets to him, Mr. Bennett stands up and shakes Bruno's hand with a genuinely happy smile on his face. Bruno's smile seems to be one of relief, like he was concerned Mr. Bennett was going to be unhappy to see him. They're making small talk when I feel someone poke me in the shoulder.

"You know who that is, right?" Tracy says, leaning over from her seat next to me. "That's Bruno Morgan. He used to go to our elementary school. He was in your boyfriend's class when his antler thing happened."

My *boyfriend*?

"You mean Andy?" I ask.

"Yeah," Tracy says. "You two are dating, right?"

"Um..." I know what I want to say, but it wouldn't have been the truth. "No. We're just friends."

"Oh. Sorry," Tracy replies rather casually. "Anyway, Bruno there stopped coming to our school after Andy freaked out at Bruno's dad and beat him with his antlers."

"He beat Bruno's dad?" I ask, surprised. I know very little about the "antler incident" but hadn't heard anyone got hurt!

"Punched him in the face or something," Tracy says. "Anyway, Bruno disappeared, and no one really heard from him 'til he moved back here, like, last November or something. I think his parents divorced or something. It was apparently super messy."

"Oh my gosh. Wait, you think that was all Andy's fault?"

"Don't know," Tracy says with a shrug. "You should ask him."

Bruno and Mr. Bennett finish their conversation, and Bruno turns to take his seat again. He looks over toward Tracy and me. He gives us a shy smile before looking down and walking back to his desk in the back.

"I wonder if he knows you and Andy are together," Tracy whispers.

"We're not together!" I snap back in a hushed tone.

"I'm sorry, I meant 'friends,'" Tracy corrects, with air quotes around "friends."

I roll my eyes.

"Seriously, though," Tracy continues, with a hint more sincerity. "Andy's actually a nice guy. And he looks like he really likes you. I bet if you asked him, he'd go out with you."

"I've tried," I admit. "But I don't think he's interested. It's okay, though. We've been friends for a while, so maybe that's it."

"Well, I'm rooting for you," Tracy says with a kind smile. "Hey, if you're not busy, come sit with us at lunch."

Wow. I'm flattered at her offer, but I don't know what to say. No one's asked me to sit with them at lunch before. Well, except Andy.

"I promise not to talk about Andy," she adds.

"Sure," I say. "Thanks."

Wow. I had no idea anyone noticed how much Andy and I

hang out together. I guess we've gotten so close as friends we don't care. We mostly hang out outside of school. We've only had one semester where our lunch schedules overlapped, and this is the first semester we don't have at least one class together. Considering the one class we would have had together was this class, it's quite fortuitous he ended up changing his mind. God only knows how well he'd have survived a class taught by his father and attended by his best friend and his elementary school bully.

Oh wait. That must have been it! Last Friday when we were getting coffee. When he started to get more quiet and give me shorter answers. When his headache started. It must have been after I brought up Bruno. I accidentally made him uncomfortable by bringing up Bruno.

I can't be too mad at myself. Andy never told me the name of his bully. But still, I hate thinking that I may have hurt him somehow. I don't like when he's sad or angry or frustrated. I wish I could be there to hold his hand when he's feeling down. Or when he's upset, give him a hug. Or when he feels like crying, give him a...

Oh God! Do I have a serious crush on Andy?

2

The Girl Who Had a Question

Rick

Abby and I sit in our individual reading chairs in the living room that evening. I read through my students' reactions to the short story I assigned them the other day. Abby has her laptop on her lap typing away. It sounds as if she has ideas flowing. Her keyboard taps warm my heart. It means she's unleashing her creativity. I'm so proud of her.

My students have begun to do the same, if these first few assignments are anything to go by.

Andy comes down from his room to get something to drink from the fridge after doing his homework, I assume. His mother and I have an agreement: give him a month before we decide we need to nag him about his schoolwork responsibilities. We should be able to tell by his grades at that point if we need to bother him.

"Hey, Dad?" he calls from the kitchen, followed by the distinct sound of a can of soda opening. "Could I get a ride from you tomorrow? I'm going to work out in the weight room after school."

"Sure thing, bud," I reply. "Meet me in my classroom when you're done?"

"Cool," he says. He starts heading back to his room.

"How's your head?" Abby asks.

"Um, fine I guess," Andy replies unconvincingly.

"Do you have a headache now?" she asks.

"Maybe a small one," Andy replies, as if getting caught with his hand in the cookie jar.

"Put the soda on the counter and get a glass of water instead," Abby orders.

Andy huffs, clearly holding back arguing with his mother. *Good choice, son.* Better to comply, even begrudgingly, than argue. He sets the can hard on the counter and grabs a glass from the cabinet.

"If your headache hasn't gone away by the end of the week, I'm making a doctor's appointment for you," Abby adds. Her statement leaves no room for negotiation.

"Whatever." Andy sighs.

"Want to try that again?" Abby sternly retorts.

Andy huffs again. "Fine. I'll let you know if my headaches don't go away."

"Damn right," Abby replies.

I watch Andy, his mother's response clearly catching him off guard, as I see him laugh and shake his head.

"Love you," Abby adds.

"Yeah, whatever, Mom," Andy says with a smile before heading back upstairs with his glass of water.

"How do you do that?" I ask my wife.

"Do what?" Abby asked.

"How do you get our reclusive teenage son to do what you ask?" I clarify. "He's supposed to be at an age where he hates us."

"I guess we've done a good job raising him," she replies.

The tone of her response makes it clear she's not entirely convinced of her own sentiment.

"He doesn't hate you," I say sincerely. "He's never hated you. You do realize that, right?"

Abby sighs. It's a worried sigh. "He doesn't have a lot of friends," she replies. "I mean, he has Joslyn, and she's been a godsend, but if he's not hanging out with her, he's home in his room. He's not socializing. He's not going out and living his life." I can hear in Abby's voice she's starting to choke up. "I just can't help but wonder, is that my fault? Because he has such a recognizable mother, he can't feel comfortable going out or hanging with friends or people his own age?"

"Oh, Abby." I get up from my chair and put my arms around my wife. She starts to weep quietly. "You shouldn't keep asking yourself those questions. You know they upset you. And you know the answer is, there is no fault to be dealt. We have an amazing life here, in no small part due to you being who you are. Our son is still figuring out who he is. And he's still dealing with events in his past. Events he surely wouldn't have been able to overcome so quickly if it wasn't for you and your love for him. He knows that. I can see it every time he interacts with you. Give him time.

He'll figure himself out. And when he needs advice, you and I will be here for him. Always."

"Thank you, my love," she says, wiping her tears. "I needed to hear that."

Joslyn

Tracy and I walk to the lunchroom after class and sit in our now-regular lunch spot. She so graciously invited me to join her cohort with Jason, Maxine, and Paul, and let me invite Lauren and Riley from my history class to join. It feels a little strange socializing with people at lunch. Well, I say socializing; I mostly listen to their conversations. They've all known each other for many years. Paul, Maxine, Riley, and Tracy all went to the same elementary school when they were younger.

And they all know Andy, too, and they all know he and I hang out a lot. That's probably why they were so open (eager maybe?) to invite me to sit with them. So they can ask how he's doing. They sound more concerned than just curious, which is nice. I wonder if Andy knows there are people concerned about him in our school.

Most of us settle into our table for lunch and commence with the usual small talk while we wait for Paul. Maxine and Jason share an anecdote about Mr. Raffman's physics class and his propensity to "run bunnies into brick walls" in his physics examples. Lauren tells us about how orchestra's going and how they're prepping again for spring concerts and competitions. She recently switched from violin to upright bass just to try it. "I'm still trying to figure out if I should stand or sit on the stool," she says.

Then Tracy notices Paul's coming, and he has someone with him. She nudges me to look over. The table gets quiet.

"Hey, guys," Paul says. "Mind if Bruno joins us today?"

"Sure," Tracy replies, smiling. "Grab a seat!"

"Thanks," Bruno says a little shyly. He places his tray on the table next to me and sits down. Everyone remains quiet, though Tracy's still smiling. It seems no one wants to break the ice.

"Hi," I say. "I'm Joslyn. We're both in Mr. Bennett's writing class." Like he didn't already know that.

"Hey," Bruno says. "Yeah, I remember seeing you. It's nice to meet you."

"So, you recently moved back here?" I ask.

A few people at the table shift a little after I ask my question, but Bruno politely answers, "Uh, yeah. My mom and I moved back from Virginia a few months ago."

"Oh, you were in Virginia?" Riley asks, a little more interested. "We wondered where you moved to. How'd you like it out there?"

"It was alright," Bruno says. "Not much going on out there, really."

The table's quiet again. I look around, and most everyone is looking at their lunches. Tracy is still smiling.

Bruno continues. "So, I guess it's been a while since I've seen you guys. How've y'all been?"

"Things are good," Tracy says, a little too anxiously. "Not too much has changed."

This actually seems to get everyone talking, as it seems a *lot* has changed since their elementary school days. The familiar burger place that was apparently popular when they were younger closed down a few years ago. The mall they grew up walking around had been renovated and stores had changed. Teachers they had in elementary school had retired. Kids they knew had moved or grown in unexpected ways.

"And Joslyn here is dating Andy," Riley says, rather randomly.

I turn to her wide-eyed. I mean, I get she's trying to add to the conversation, but why say that?

Tracy quickly interjects on my behalf. "They're not dating, they're just friends."

"Really?" Riley says confused. "But you guys hang out all the time. You're practically joined at the hip."

I feel my cheeks start to burn.

"No," Tracy corrects more emphatically, hoping Riley gets the hint. "They're just friends."

Riley looks at me, even more confused, but at least she has the good sense to keep her follow-up questions to herself as I'm trying to hide my face from everyone. I can't believe she said that!

There's a beat of silence, then Bruno says, "How is Andy doing?"

I look up and realize he's asking me. And he sounds genuinely interested.

"Um," I start, "he's good. I mean, I don't know what he was like when you knew him..." I see Bruno's expression turn sad as I say this. He looks almost guilty. I'd forgotten Tracy told me Bruno was Andy's bully in elementary school. "But he's doing alright," I say. "He's taking all the art classes. Started weightlifting last semester. Normal stuff."

Wait, is that actually "normal stuff"?

"That's good to hear," Bruno replies, a little relieved. "How long have you two been friends?"

"Since eighth grade," I say. "We met in art class. I inadvertently confessed that I was a big fan of one of his mom's movies, but we...I mean, it worked out."

"That's nice," Bruno says kindly. He smiles at me, and I can just feel Tracy scowl just a little. "I'm really glad to hear he's doing alright. I haven't seen him since I got back. I hope I get the nerve to walk up to him and say hi at some point."

"You haven't talked to him?" Tracy asks. "You talked to his dad after class the other day."

"Yeah, and I was scared as hell to do that," Bruno explains. "I had no idea he was our teacher for that class when I signed up. Had I known, I probably would've picked something else." Bruno chuckles nervously.

Everyone else shifts in their seats.

I don't say anything.

"Um," Tracy starts to say quietly, "you still speak with your dad at all?"

Bruno goes quiet. His eyes darken a little. Everyone shifts again. I don't say anything.

"Not really," he finally says. "Found out he'd been screwing my mom on child support a few years ago, and I just decided to cut him off. Like my mom says, I don't need that kind of negativity in my life, y'know?"

I feel sorry for Bruno. I know he was a bully back in elementary school, but no one should suffer with a bad father. I look around the table again. Everyone looks like they feel sorry for him too.

Paul smiles and pats Bruno on the back. "Your mom's right, dude," he says. "Your dad was an asshole, and you don't need to be dealing with that."

Everyone murmurs words of agreement. Bruno smiles and kinda chuckles. He then looks at me as if he wants to apologize for making everything awkward. I just smile and shrug. It's all good with me.

Tracy then brings up someone else they went to elementary school with, and everyone again starts talking about more people they knew, how people are doing according to their social media posts, and so on. I just listen, and so does Bruno. I think he's still a little nervous sitting with everyone. But he seems like a nice guy.

It's about five minutes to the end of lunch, and we all start to get up and get ready to head to our afternoon classes. I pick up my bag to leave when Bruno asks if I could hang back for a moment to talk to me in private. I say, "Sure," and we wait for everyone else to leave.

"Listen," he starts. I can tell he's really nervous. "I don't know how much Andy's talked about me or anything, but I...I just wanted you to know, seeing as how you're his friend, that I'm really sorry."

"Sorry for what?" I asked.

"I was a real bully to him when we were kids," Bruno confesses, "and I deserved a lot of what I got out of it. So did my dad. In case I don't get a chance to tell him that, could you tell him I said that?"

So did his dad? What happened to them when they were kids?

"I could try," I offer, "but don't you think you should tell him? If this is about the antler incident, he actually hasn't told me a whole lot about it. He doesn't really like to talk about it with me."

Bruno looks at me a little confused. "He doesn't?"

I shake my head.

"Why not?"

I just shrug. Bruno doesn't need to know about Andy's second antler incident.

"Well, I guess you're right," Bruno admits. "About talking to Andy myself, I mean. I'll try and talk to him at some point."

I nod in agreement.

"Maybe you can tell him he, at least, has good taste in not-girlfriend friends."

I blush a little. "Maybe that's what I'll call myself," I reply, trying to sound casual. "Andy's not-girlfriend."

"But y'know," Bruno adds, "if you like him like that, you should tell him."

What? I look at Bruno surprised as I feel my cheeks heat up again.

Just then, the bell rings, and Bruno throws his backpack over his shoulder. "See you in class tomorrow," he says before walking out of the cafeteria.

I just stand there for a second, completely stunned.

Is it really that obvious?

That I don't actually want to be Andy's not-girlfriend?

Andy

Mom suggested I look for different outlets other than drawing and screaming into pillows any time I feel frustrated. My therapist suggested I look for physical outlets, like running or exercise. I tried running for a while, but my feet kept falling asleep after ten minutes, so I switched to weightlifting. I didn't realize just how many muscles I had in my arms alone until I started working out regularly.

I really enjoy working out, especially with the punching bag. It's been a much better way to let out my frustrations. I thought about asking my parents to get me one for Christmas last year, but I don't trust Dad to attach it to my bedroom ceiling securely. Mom would be pissed if the ceiling collapsed because of a poorly installed punching bag.

I pull out my phone to check the time and see if Joslyn's texted at all. It's 3:30, but I haven't gotten any texts. That's odd. I usually have at least one text from her by this time after school, asking how my day went or something. She's always asking me how my day went. I don't think I've ever texted her that first. I should probably start doing that. I'll send her a message when I get to Dad's classroom.

I run my head under the sink for a quick wash in the locker room before changing and heading to dad's room. The door's closed when I get there, which is a little strange, as Dad has a literal open-door policy with his students. I knock a few times before I open the door, only to see Joslyn's there talking with Dad. They both look at me and suddenly go silent. Jos looks...upset.

"Hey," I say, stepping into the room. "What's up?"

"Hey, bud," Dad says. "Come on in. Joslyn and I were just chatting."

"No problem," I say, entering the classroom and putting my things down by the door. "I wasn't expecting to see you here, Jos. Everything alright?"

"It's fine," she says in her short-word tone. I may be new to understanding some of the nuances in talking to girls, but I know Jos is not fine.

"Um, you sure?" I ask, trying not to sound like a complete dick about it.

"Yeah," she says, looking away from me. "I was actually about to head home."

"Oh, you want me to walk with you?" I offer. "I was going to get a ride with Dad, but I can walk with you if you want."

"No, I'm fine," she replies, clearly not fine. "Thanks, though."

"Alright," I say, confused and concerned. "I guess I'll text you later then?"

"Sure," she says. She then looks at Dad. "Thanks for letting me ask my questions." She gets up with her things and finally looks at me again. She gives me a small smile before walking past me out of the room.

"Bye," I say behind her. She doesn't turn around. I turn to Dad. "What's going on? Is she okay? What happened?" I feel myself getting angry. "Did someone hurt Joslyn? Did someone make fun of her looks again?"

"Joslyn's fine," Dad says in his "please stay calm" voice. "She apparently had lunch with Bruno today and she had some...questions."

Oh no... "What did you tell her?"

"I told her the truth," Dad says.

Dammit! I huff and throw my hands in the air. I turn away from Dad.

"I told her the truth from my perspective," he continues. "About how Bruno's dad attempted to take credit for my script and how we found out and how that was the impetus to the antler incident."

I growl in frustration. I actually growl! What the hell, Dad?

"Andy, why didn't you tell her what happened that day?"

"I did!" I retort. "I told her after I freaked her out and grew antlers."

"But you didn't give her all the details," Dad replies.

"Well, I didn't expect Bruno to show up again! Or, I guess, have a class with her and sit with her at lunch. And besides, it's kinda none of her business what I did or how it happened. I'm not that kid anymore."

"I beg to differ," Dad says.

"What does that mean?"

Dad gives me a look.

I get angry. "No, really. Do you think it's her business? Or are you saying I'm still a kid?"

"Andy, you need to calm yourself."

I huff again. Dammit, now my head is pounding.

"You're getting a headache again."

"Yeah, well, whose fault is that?"

"Andy, you need to calm down, and you need to face your real frustration."

"Yeah? And what's that?"

"That you care about Joslyn!"

I look at my dad in complete shock. "Of course, I care for Jos," I say defensively. "She's my best friend. Who doesn't care about their best friend?"

"You know what I mean," Dad says, folding his arms.

I huff and turn away again.

"You care a great deal about her, and she clearly cares a great deal about you. The least you could do is admit it to yourself. Hell, it's why you've been suffering so many headaches."

"No, you not telling me Bruno was back in town was giving me a headache," I retort. God, my head is killing me.

Dad takes a long breath and closes his eyes. "I might deserve some of that," he admits. "Look, as a father watching his son in pain, I'm not going to stand by and just let you wallow in this. Maybe I'm wrong about your feelings for Jos, and if so, forgive my temerity." Ugh, Dad and his ten-dollar words again. "But something is wrong, something you are fighting to face. And it's hurting you. Literally hurting you. We can't help you if you're not going to help yourself."

I don't respond. Dad's right. I definitely have a lot going on. Joslyn asked me out, and I don't have an answer for her. Bruno reappeared out of the blue, and I'm not ready to deal with him. All I've been doing is arguing with Dad and beating up a punching bag. I reached up to feel the top of my head. No antlers, but my head is pounding again.

"You're right, Dad," I say, letting out a breath. "I'm sorry. I don't know what's going on with me right now."

"It's not obvious?" Dad says with a half-smile. "You're growing up, that's what's going on."

3

⌘

The Boy Who Tried and the Girl Who Cried

Andy

I sit at my regular corner table at lunch trying to sketch out mountain landscapes in the new style I'd told Jos I wanted to try for the battle scene in our story. I'm hoping to show her some ideas after school today.

I've been trying to keep my head down at lunch, but people still insist on waving and saying "Hey!" as they walk past me. A few weeks ago, some freshman named Julio and his buddies decided it would be funny to taunt me from a few tables away. They were laughing, then turning over their shoulders and calling out, "Hey, Antler Boy! You wanna show us how big you are, Antler Boy?"

I honestly don't know where they got off doing that. I don't even know how they found out! Ever since high school started, no one's bothered me about that stuff. A few guys I knew from way back in elementary school overheard Julio and his buddies taunting me and told them to knock it off. It wasn't a suggestion either. I think it might've freaked the freshmen out, because Julio stopped after that. Not completely though. Every once and a while I'll hear someone call out "Antler Boy" behind me, then snicker. I just take out my frustrations on the punching bag. Like I said to Dad the other day, I have a lot going on.

I hear snickering from the table a few feet away. I glance up from my tablet. Dammit, Julio and his friends are sitting a few tables away again. They're looking over their shoulders and laughing, looking for the right opportunity to call out that amazingly unoriginal taunt. Ugh. Not today, guys. Seriously, I'm not in the mood.

Before they can even call once, however, Mike and Sal come up to my table.

"Hey, man," Sal says. "Mind if we join you?"

Mike and Sal were the ones who shut those freshmen down last time. Least I can do is let them sit with me. "Go ahead," I say, moving my tray closer to me to give them room to sit.

"Thanks," Sal says. He glances over at the other table.

Julio and the others turn back around. Their table goes quiet.

"Hope you don't mind us putting those jerks in their place for you," Sal says.

"Yeah," Mike adds. "They shouldn't be saying that stuff to you. It's uncool."

"Yeah, thanks for looking out for me," I say. "I appreciate it. Really, that's awesome, you guys."

We start making small talk, mostly about our classes. It's all pretty chill. I've known Mike and Sal since elementary school. We occasionally have a class or two together, but we've never really hung out. They're good guys, though. Even though they were in my class when the antler incident happened, they never made a big deal out of it. They might've been frightened by it at first, but even still, they stayed cool. I probably should've thanked them for that by now.

"So, we saw Bruno's back," Mike says. "How're you feeling about that? Have you talked to him?"

"Nah," I say, trying not to sound bothered. "Not yet, at least. We're not in any classes together. I maybe saw him once in the hall, but I haven't talked to him."

"Isn't he in that class your dad's teaching, with your girlfriend?" Sal asks. "Joslyn, right?"

"Yeah," I reply. "It's no big deal."

"So," Mike starts, leaning in a little, "how long have you and Jos been dating?"

"What?" I say, surprised. "We're not dating."

"But you just said she was your girlfriend," Mike says.

"I did?" I say, confused. "No, she's just my friend. And a girl. So girl-friend, right?"

Mike and Sal laugh. "Yeah, whatever you say, man," Mike says, putting about six tater tots in his mouth.

"Shut up," I say, defensively. I try to go back to drawing on my template. I feel my cheeks getting warm. Dammit, I should've been paying more attention to what they were saying. Now I'm embarrassed.

"It's all good," Sal says reassuringly. "He's not trying to tease you. But Jos is a cute girl. You don't take the chance soon, some-one else is gonna ask her to the spring dance."

I just murmur, "Whatever," and continue trying to draw and not blush.

"Oh," Sal says, "I wanted to ask. You're doing weight training with Coach D after school, yeah? How's that going? I was think-ing of checking it out."

I talk about the gym on campus, tell them my experience with working with the weights and using the punching bags. We actually have a pretty good conversation. Sal's looking to improve his ab game and Mike, well, he continues to eat his tater tots, but he listens anyway. I can't remember the last time I sat with anyone at lunch and chatted about this stuff. I didn't usually talk to Jos about working out. We're always talking about our creative ideas. It's actually been kinda lonely without her at lunch.

As the guys and I continue to talk muscle groups, I keep think-ing I kinda miss having lunch with Jos. I mean, I'm enjoying the chat with Sal and Mike, but I miss just being with her. Sometimes she would be writing, and I would be drawing, and we wouldn't even talk, but it was all good. Great, even. Being in her company. Though, y'know, I think if she saw me now, chatting with Sal and Mike at lunch, she'd be proud of me. She'd be happy to see I'm socializing, making friends like she's been able to do. Sure, maybe I wasn't happy to hear she has lunch with Bruno now, but it's not just the two of them. She sits with, like, five or six people now. That makes me happy to think she's not alone.

I hope I'll remember to tell Jos all this at our next coffee hang.

But that won't be today. Joslyn asked this morning if we could cancel our Friday coffee meetup for this afternoon. She said she had a lot more homework this week than she had anticipated and wanted to get a head start on it. I wanted to say that we still could get coffee anyway, even if it was a quick one, but I didn't. I just said that it wasn't a problem and told her I'd text her later tonight. She texted back *OK :)* and we left it at that.

I wonder if her conversation with Dad really upset her that much. Maybe I won't text her tonight. Or maybe I will text her just to say that I think it's okay if she wants some space. and we can take the weekend off and talk again on Monday.

Unless she *wants* to talk. Or is waiting for me to talk to her. Dad's right, I do owe her some explanations. It wasn't as big a deal until Bruno came back, and I can't blame him for returning after all this time.

But still, I can't face him yet either. I'm not ready yet. I haven't prepared myself. Or really, I didn't prepare myself because I was too busy enjoying my time hanging out with Jos.

Man, do I enjoy hanging out with her. She's so smart and clever. And I love all the books she recommends. Dad was so surprised when he saw I was reading. He gave that cliché, "Where's my real son?" response. Jos laughed when I told her that.

We find video games we both like and play them for hours. I love how proud she looks when she's beaten me fair and square.

And her laugh is so cute too. Man, do I love to make her laugh. And she has the cutest smile. I remember when we held hands when we were at the *Grace Falls* rerelease event a few years ago. We haven't held hands since then. I actually kinda miss holding her hand. I never thought I'd miss something like that. I wonder if maybe, someday, she'll let me hold her hand again.

And, y'know, if it'll make her happy, I'll go to the spring dance with her. I'll be her date. Actually, now that I think about it, that doesn't sound like a bad idea. I'll be able to hold her hand, and we'll be able to slow dance together. I wonder if she's ever had a slow dance before. I wonder how close she'll let me hold her. And maybe at the end of the night when I bring her home, she'll let me give her a...

Oh, man, I *do* have a serious crush on Joslyn!

I can't tell her now. I need to give her time to get over things. But when is the right time to tell her? I guess I don't have to tell her everything right away. I could start by telling her that I'll go to the spring dance with her. That is, if she still wants to go with me. If I haven't upset her too much. Maybe I'll ask her on Monday. In person. It's probably better if I ask in person rather than text.

Thinking about asking Joslyn to the spring dance makes me feel a whole lot better. I can't even feel a headache coming on or anything. My head's totally fine. This is great! I can't wait to get home and tell Mom! Mom worries about me so much, I bet she'll feel so much better when she hears I had a good day today, and that I'm planning on asking Joslyn out to the dance.

I get home and take my shoes off in the foyer. I think I hear Mom on the back porch. I go to check before heading upstairs to drop off my stuff.

She's sitting in one of the hammock chairs Gramma got us for Christmas. It sounds like Mom's on the phone. And...

Is she crying?

I quietly sit down on the couch in the living room and listen.

"Yeah, I'm surprised at myself too," I hear her say. "I know he was just being honest in his critiques. I mean, he wasn't wrong.

What I wrote wasn't all that great. I don't know why it hit me so hard."

That's right. I almost forgot, Mom had asked Dad to read the story she was writing for fun. I'm sure it wasn't that bad, but Dad also isn't going to lie if something he's asked to read could be better.

"Well, that's the other thing," Mom continues, "it's still just a first draft. It's supposed to need improvements. ... No, he just sent it today when he was on his lunch break. He's not home yet. ... I don't know. I was kinda hoping that talking to you would calm me down before he gets home. He doesn't need to see me crying, especially when he's already worried about me. ... No, it's just, it's just old wounds, I guess."

Dad told me once, the sound of Mom crying was the one sound he never wants to hear. Not to mean Mom shouldn't cry when she's upset, only that he doesn't like seeing Mom upset. As I think about it, I kinda feel the same way about Joslyn. The thought of Jos being upset enough to cry, it hurts a little.

I keep listening.

"Hey, Mom, how did you deal with me when I started going to school? Were you worried I wasn't going to make friends? ... Well, you were still on TV at the time. ... Seriously? You weren't worried? ... Well, I don't know if it was that easy for me. You have to remember, though, I started acting at fourteen, and Andy's just a few months away from turning seventeen. ... Oh, don't remind me. I'm still in denial. He's still my baby boy."

I chuckle to myself. If I was younger, I would have been so much more embarrassed to hear her say that.

"He's alright," Mom says. "He's been having some pain around the top of his head. I suspect it's legacy pains from his antlers, but he hasn't talked about it much to me. ... No, I trust he'll tell me when it gets bad. I figured I'd give Dr. Reinholdt a call and make an appointment."

Mom goes on to talk about our vacation up to Washington, mountain biking and seeing the snow, before it sounds like Gramma has to go, and she hangs up the call. When she comes into the house, she sees me sitting on the couch. I'm just looking at her.

"Oh, welcome home," Mom says, somewhat surprised to see me. She puts on a smile to look like she hasn't been crying, but her eyes are still red. "I didn't think you'd be home this early. Did you have an okay day?"

I don't answer. I just stand up from the couch and give Mom a great big hug.

Right now, I think we both need a hug.

Joslyn

The weekend is too quiet. I haven't heard from Andy once since I canceled our coffee on Friday.

I bet he thinks I'm mad at him. Maybe he'll be up to chat after school today.

I guess I'm a little upset with him after my conversation with his dad last Wednesday. I was so grateful Mr. Bennett offered to talk to me when I asked what happened between Andy and Bruno, or rather Andy and Bruno's dad. I'd heard of Dylan Morgan; I knew him from the few movies he was in with Miss Abby many years ago. He later moved on to work on animated cartoons. He'd produced a few of the cartoons I watched growing up, and at the time, I wanted to learn more about what a cartoon producer did, so I researched Morgan's career. That's when I learned that, about six years ago, he was unceremoniously fired from Reimagine Productions for plagiarism and accusations of sexual harassment. It took me a while to go back to watching some of those movies and shows. There're still a few things I can't watch anymore.

I had no idea that some of the work Morgan attempted to steal belonged to Andy's dad. And the day he and Andy happened to find out was the day of the antler incident. And Bruno and all the people I now hang out with at lunch watched it all go down. That must have been so traumatizing. I did my best to withhold my questions for Bruno at lunch the next day. I bet none of our growing cohort knows all the details.

I wonder why Mr. Bennett shared all this with me, and why Andy didn't. Maybe Andy thought this was none of my business.

But I haven't spoken much with Andy since then. Just a few chats, mostly canceling coffee. Then nothing over the weekend. I didn't even have the chance to tell him that I had been having lunch with Bruno, and that Bruno seems like a good guy and that I think the two of them should talk again.

I can't wait any longer. I text Andy at lunch and ask if he can meet me after school. Other than hoping we could clear the air on things, I really just miss talking with him. Even though I've been making friends and having wonderful conversations at lunch now, I miss chatting with Andy.

I miss asking him how his day went, if he has any new ideas for our story, what homework is frustrating him the most, and if I can help.

I miss hearing him get all animated when he's describing a drawing he wants to do, or something he's seen on TV or played in his video game that he just can't wait to share.

I miss complaining about how we have to look for jobs this summer.

It had only really been four days, and I miss Andy.

Oh God, I *do* have a serious crush on him.

I know I'm not going to get a message back from him for a little while, since he has sixth period lunch while I have fourth period lunch, but still, I'm super anxious. Fifth and sixth period classes are practically a blur. My stomach starts to churn. I'm actually starting to feel sick.

Different scenarios go through my head: What if he doesn't answer me before school lets out? Do I just wait? Do I go looking for him? Do I go home? Or, what if he can't meet or doesn't want to meet today? Would I be able to wait until tomorrow? I've never thought about these things before. I've certainly never felt this kind of anxiety before.

The more I think about it, the more outrageous my thoughts become: What if I've been reading things all wrong? What if he actually doesn't like me the same way I like him? Am I about to ruin things just by wanting to talk to him? What if I find out he actually doesn't care, and finding out that I like him—like, *like* like him—will ruin our entire friendship?

Then, just as sixth period is about to wrap up, I feel my phone vibrate in my bag. I lean down and peek in, trying to look inconspicuous.

I've never felt so happy to see a text in my entire life:

*Hey! I really want to talk to you too! I was going to show
a couple guys the weight room after school. Can you meet me
at Jordan Park at about 2:30?*

Completely ignoring school rules or any better judgment, I reach into my bag and send my response:

Yes! See you then :)

I'll never have a better seventh period history class in my life. As if by magic or divine intervention, a simple phone buzz and text message evaporates all my anxiety. If I'm anxious about anything now, it's for school to end so I can get to Jordan Park.

The 1:55 bell rings and I pack myself up fast, rush to my locker to get the rest of my things, and leave the school ready to head to...

Wait, how do I get to Jordan Park? I've never been there. I pull out my phone and try to search it in my map app. Unfortunately, the search just keeps spinning. Why is my signal so crappy right here, right now? I pinch in the map to see if it will load faster. Nope, that doesn't work. I zoom the map out and... Dammit, now it's too far back! Why can't I get this to work? I have to get there before Andy does or he'll think I ditched him. I should've asked for directions when he texted me earlier. Damn my phone!

"Hey, Joslyn," I hear a voice call from behind me.

I turn around quickly. Maybe a little too quickly.

Bruno jumps back a step. "Whoa! Everything all right? You look like you're about to scream."

"It's my phone," I say. "It's not loading the map. I told Andy

I'd meet him at Jordan Park, but I...I don't know how to get there from here."

"Oh," Bruno says, "I know how to get to Jordan Park. I can walk you there, if you'd like."

"That would be so awesome," I say with great relief. "As long as it's no trouble."

"No problem," Bruno replies happily. "Come with me."

Andy

I finish exchanging contact information with Sal and Mike before I head out to meet Jos at Jordan Park. I can't believe how stupid happy I was when I saw her text today about meeting up. I actually found myself rereading it a few times, as if I needed to be reminded that she isn't upset with me.

Hey Andy. Would you be able to meet up after school today? I was hoping we could talk. Let me know!

I didn't see the message until I got to lunch with the guys. I'm so excited I show the guys. I explain how I saw Jos talking with Dad about the antler incident and how we hadn't really talked since.

"You don't think she wants to break up with you or something?" Mike asks with a chuckle.

Sal slaps him on the back of the head. "They're not dating!"

"I was actually thinking I'd ask Joslyn to the spring dance if she still wanted," I say.

"Still?" both Sal and Mike ask at the same time.

I rub the back of my neck. "Yeah, she kinda hinted that she wanted to go with me last week, and I missed the hint."

"Do it!" Mike insists. "Totally ask her to the dance!"

"I think you should too," Sal adds. "She makes you happy. You make her happy. What's wrong with that?"

"Are...are you guys dating anyone?" I ask, a little embarrassed. I feel like I should know this already.

"Nah," Mike says dismissively. "All the girls I like are way out of my league. I'll wait for college."

"Sal?"

"I tried to date this girl freshman year, but it didn't work out," Sal admits. "But there is a girl in orchestra I was thinking of asking to the spring dance. She just switched from violin to upright bass, and I'm trying to help teach her. She's always been super nice, but I don't know if she's seeing anyone, so I'm not sure how to ask."

"You could just ask," Mike says. "Can't read minds, so might as well ask."

"I need to get back to Joslyn here," I say, pulling out my phone again. "Oh shoot! I was going to show you guys the weight room today, wasn't I?" I look at Jos's message again. I really want to meet with her, but...

"Actually," I say, coming up with an idea. "I can make this work. I'll ask if she can meet me at Jordan Park at, like, 2:30. That'll give me a few minutes to show you guys around and maybe get myself psyched up to ask her out. Plus, the park's nicer than a high school parking lot."

"Jordan Park!" Mike says. "Oh, man, do you guys remember that playground? All made of wood and tires and stuff. Such a bummer when they tore it all out and replaced it with the boring metal stuff.”

“I loved climbing the trees,” Sal says.

“Me too!” I exclaim. “Dude, we should totally do rock climbing someday.”

“Oh, man, that would be great!”

We keep chatting about the park, climbing trees, and rock climbing for another ten minutes before I realize I haven't sent the text to Jos yet! Gotta send this quick, before lunch period ends.

Hey! I really want to talk to you too! I was going to show a couple guys the weight room after school. Can you meet me at Jordan Park at about 2:30?

We pack up our stuff and pile our trash to throw away when I feel my phone buzz in my hand.

Yes! See you then :)

I hold up my phone and show it to the guys. “See?” I say. “Smiley face. She doesn't want to break up with me.” The guys and I laugh.

* * *

I try my best to keep myself composed and to take my time getting to the park. I keep thinking about what I want to say.

Should I start with some apology? Some recognition that something I did or didn't do or say or didn't say may've upset her? I suppose if I'm going to apologize, I probably should at least figure out what I need to apologize for.

Should I try and bring up something about how I feel about her? How much I really do like her and how great a friend she is? How much I enjoy our time together, how I think she's cute, how I like her laugh, how...

That's definitely too much. I don't want to make it sound like a marriage proposal. This is just the spring dance. It's not even prom!

Also, I'm still not sure what these feelings I have for her are. I should probably figure that out, too, before I say anything.

Why not keep it simple? Say something like, "I'm sorry I missed what you were asking before. I'd like to go to the spring dance with you." But what if I'm even getting that wrong? I mean, I never really did confirm that was what she was asking. On the chance that wasn't it, then that kind of thing just sounds presumptuous.

No, I'll have to keep it more simple. The most simple. Something like, "Would you like to go to the spring dance with me?" That's it. That's all it has to be. I can do this. I think I can do this.

I'm at the final intersection and crosswalk before entering the park, waiting for the light to change, and I start feeling butterflies and knots in my stomach. Oh God, I'm getting anxious. Maybe this isn't so bad. Maybe this feeling is affirmation that I'm doing the right thing, that these feelings I have are, well, the right feelings to have.

I just hope she has the same feelings for me, or this will be really awkward.

The light changes and I make my way across the street toward the park. There's an open space with a bunch of benches, and I assume that's where I'll be able to find Joslyn. I suppose I should have clarified a specific spot. If I don't see her past 2:30, I'll just text her.

I walk down the path and hear steps coming up behind me, rushing quickly. I turn to look over my shoulder. Maybe it's Jos trying to catch up.

Just then, a pebble hits me just above my right eye. "Ow!" I wince and grab my forehead. Who the hell threw that?

"Aaaantler Boy."

No. Not here. Not now.

They're laughing and pointing. Julio and his goons. One of them has a few small rocks in his palm. I watch as he picks another from his hand and chucks it in my direction. I flinch, throwing my arms in front of my face to block the hit.

"What the hell, man?" I call out. "What's wrong with you?"

"What?" Julio teases. "You too chicken to come at me?"

"C'mon, bro!" another of his gang calls out. "Grow them!"

Another rock hits my face. This one stings. I reach up and touch my face. Blood.

"Leave me the hell alone!" I snap. "What the hell is your problem?"

"Oh," Julio continues to taunt. "The freak don't wanna fight me. Antler Boy don't know how to grow his horns. Guess whose is bigger now?"

Another rock comes flying at my face. I turn, and the rock hits the side of my head. I curse under my breath and just start to walk away. I'm not looking for a fight.

"Oh look," Julio calls out. "He's probably runnin' off to find his Cabbage Patch."

I stop. I turn around again. "What did you say?" I demand. He'd better not be talking about who I think he's talking about.

"That chick you're always with," Julio says, laughing. "With the patchy skin. Your Cabbage Patch. You runnin' off to her? You runnin' off to cry?"

My blood is boiling. I walk straight up to Julio and get right in his face. "You," I say, anger dripping in my words, "will never call her that again, you hear me?"

"Or what?" Julio says, getting more in my face. "You gonna cry and run away?"

I see him glance over my shoulder. A nasty smile grows on his face. "Looks like she's got another dude anyway, bro."

What is he talking about? I turn around. There's Joslyn.
With Bruno.

Red. I'm seeing red. In all my years dealing with anger, my outbursts of rage, in this single moment I am beyond furious. Julio and his gang provoking me to fight. Bruno standing there with Joslyn. And Joslyn watching it all. Dear God, I hope she didn't hear what this bastard just called her.

"What're you gonna do, Antler Boy?" Julio says with a threatening tone.

I turn back to him. I look at him with my rage-filled eyes. I watch as his expression falls from pride to shock. He isn't prepared for this. He isn't prepared for me. For what I'm about to do.

My head is pounding.

I'm only focused on Julio. His one buddy drops the rest of the rocks in his hand while his other takes a few steps backward.

With one quick motion, I swing my right fist square into Julio's nose. He staggers backward, grasping at his face before hunching over in pain. His buddies gather at his side. I can hear him cursing me behind his hands. He opened his hands once, and I see the trickle of blood dripping from one finger. He looks back up at me and screams profanities before he and his buddies bolt from the park.

I turn back around. Joslyn's covering her mouth, clearly in shock. Tears start to stream down her cheeks. I look over at Bruno. He's also shocked. On instinct, I reach for my head. Nothing. There's nothing there. I haven't grown antlers.

Just a pounding headache.

I can't look at them anymore. I can't be there. I turn back around and walk away as quickly as I can. I need to get away from them. My head is pounding so hard my ears are ringing. My right hand starts to feel sore. I hear Joslyn call my name, but I don't turn around. I can't look at her. I just have to get out of here.

I ruined the moment. I ruined what was supposed to be my redeeming moment. I ruined it with anger. Ugly anger. In front of Joslyn. Again.

There's no way Joslyn will ever want to speak to me again.

My anger ruined everything.

Again.

4

❧

The Girl Who Saved the World

Joslyn

"Miss Harper? Would you mind staying for a moment?" Mr. Bennett asks me just after dismissing everyone for lunch.

"Sure," I say as I collect my bags. I tell Tracy to go on to lunch without me and approach Mr. Bennett, who's still standing at his desk.

"I actually have a class matter to discuss with you," he starts, "but first, I wanted to check and make sure you're alright. Andy told us what happened yesterday."

"Yeah," I say, trying to offer a little smile. "I'm fine. That was..." I actually don't want to talk about what happened yesterday. Not with Andy's dad, at least. "Well, it just was. How's Andy doing? He's not mad that I didn't text him yesterday?"

"No, he's not upset with you," Mr. Bennett assures me. "He's probably told you, but he's been suffering some substantial headaches lately."

Andy hasn't told me, but I don't say anything.

Mr. Bennett continues. "Abby's taking him to the doctor today.

"Good," I say. "Tell him...actually, never mind."

"I agree," Mr. Bennett says with a smile. "*You* should tell him."

I smile.

"With that, I did want to talk to you about your most recent assignment, Miss 451."

My eyes grow wide, and I feel my cheeks get warm. "You...you figured out which was my BA assignment?"

"Almost immediately," Mr. Bennett replies with a little shrug. "And really, it's your own fault. When the subject of a piece of work is so clearly the son of the teacher, of course I'm going to figure it out."

I sigh through my nose and look down a little ashamed.

"I mean no disrespect to you or your classmates," he tries to reassure me. "I should've figured an average high school student's allegory is pretty transparent."

What? I'm confused and I furrow my brow.

"I mean your symbolism is obvious. I'm betting I'll be able to figure out every student before the end of the semester. Literally, in fact. I have a bet with several faculty in the English department. The betting pool in the English department has a 60/80 spread apparently." He smiles. He's trying to make me feel better. It actually kinda works.

"So, do I need to write something different?" I ask. "Athea is one of the characters from the story Andy and I are working on. I was really hoping to use this class to develop her."

"Well, can I give you some advice?" Mr. Bennett asks. I nod. "Perhaps, instead of writing an epic about how she saved the life of her obvious future love interest, have her discover *herself* first. Write her a backstory—where she came from, what makes her think the way she thinks, where her motivations come from."

I nod in agreement. That's a very good idea, actually. And sounds like fun.

"Also, if I may," Mr. Bennett adds, "perhaps think of a better title than 'The Girl Who Saved the World'? Seems a little...too on the nose."

"I guess I can try," I say with a little laugh.

"That's all I had," he says. "Well, that, and also, I wanted to thank you for caring about Andy so much."

I feel myself flush.

"You have been such a great presence in his life, and reading your story it's clear you really care about him immensely. So much so you wanted to 'save his life' as it were."

I laugh nervously. "Thank you. And yeah, I do like Andy. A lot. And I'll tell him soon."

Mr. Bennett smiles very kindly. He can totally see my whole face is blushing. How can he not?

We stand there smiling for a few awkward seconds of silence. It's starting to feel weird, so I ask, "Do you have any thoughts on a better title for my story?"

"Are you kidding?" Mr. Bennett asks, holding back laughter. "I wrote a piece called, *The Boy Who Grew Antlers*, remember? What do I know about coming up with good titles?"

Abby

My poor baby boy.

When he came home yesterday, he looked like he'd killed a man. He told us some kids from his school had thrown rocks at him, trying to provoke a reaction. The blood from the cuts on his face had dried and had looked a sight. I asked if he wanted help cleaning himself up. I didn't expect him to accept my offer, but he did.

I cleaned up his face and treated his cuts. All the while, he confessed to everything—confronting the bullies as he did, defending their horrible name calling of both him and Joslyn, the shock and rage he felt seeing Joslyn with Bruno, and his ultimate response of punching his antagonizer in the nose. He promised to submit to any repercussions, but I told him not to worry about any of that now. His priority was to heal.

His father and I, of course, immediately forgave him. We knew the situation had the potential to be much worse for everyone involved. I then messaged Monica to check on Joslyn and let her know what happened, in case Joslyn hadn't already informed her. Monica assured me Joslyn was fine and that they were all mostly concerned with Andy's wellbeing. I told her how much that meant to us and that we would be in touch soon.

I brought Andy to Dr. Reinholdt's office this afternoon. Dr. Reinholdt specializes in pain and injuries related to bodily transformations, in particular legacy pains.

"Legacy pains," he explained to Andy, "are primarily psychological. It's your brain reminding your body that you had something there that you probably shouldn't have. Bodily transformations, as you can imagine, are not exactly natural. And they don't happen without a certain amount of intent by the person. Rarely is the intent unknown. Arguably, when you first grew your antlers, you must've knowingly wanted them, right?"

"I had a dream about them the night before," Andy said.

"Exactly," Dr. Reinholdt replied. "As your mother here will tell you, Muses who suffer legacy pains mostly suffer them because they're reliving a moment, event, or even a trauma in their life. That traumatic or visceral memory, when it's particularly strong or intense, can manifest as physical pain at the point of original transformation. Hence your headaches."

"And what should I do to treat it so it goes away?" Andy asked.

"Well," Dr. Reinholdt said, "what I don't particularly want to do is prescribe pain medication and hope for the best, because what we really don't want is for you to become reliant on painkillers. With that said, ibuprofen will absolutely help mitigate the pain so you can at least get some rest and get to sleep at night. Other than that, you may need to consider seeking out the help from a therapist."

We're driving home from his appointment now. The ride was silent at first. I'm proud of Andy for talking to the doctor and taking the appointment seriously. My greatest fear was he would remain silent or give noncommittal answers.

We pull up to a stoplight, and the soft rumble of the engine makes the silence louder. We both must be feeling the weight of the silence, because Andy turns to me and says, "I just want you to know, Mom, I definitely don't blame you."

My heart aches a little, but I hold it in. "I know, sweetheart," I say assuredly. "But thank you."

"I overheard you talking to Gramma last week, and I just wanted to say that to you," he says.

"Thank you." This time I can't hide the crack in my voice.

The light changes and we continue driving.

"I, um...this might be a weird question," Andy says, "but you used to say that I was your 'world.' Why did you say that?"

I smile. "Because you are," I say. I realize just how utterly cliché that is to say, as does Andy, who huffs slightly in frustration from my non-answer. I continue. "Your father and I, early in our marriage, planned to have lots of kids. I wanted to get pregnant almost immediately after we got married. But I was already under contract to work on acting projects in which I could not be pregnant. The first seven years of our marriage, I was just constantly working when all I wanted was to be having babies with your father."

"Was that hard on your marriage?" he asks gingerly.

"A little," I admit. "But it was hard because we wanted to make each other happy. Your father, as you know, is a hopeless romantic. He would say I was his 'world' all the time. And he meant it, in his own way.

"When we found out we were pregnant with you, we were unbelievably happy. Then..." I catch myself choking up at the memory. "Well, I had a few complications. There was a while during the pregnancy when we were seriously afraid that we were going to lose the pregnancy. Lose you."

I take a second to wipe my tears with the back of my hand. I glance over at Andy. He's still listening.

"I was in so much pain," I continue, "and I couldn't do much more than lie there and hope things didn't get worse. And I mean everything hurt. My back, my sides, my ankles. Hell, my ears even started to hurt."

Andy chuckles a little at that.

"And then we had you, and we never felt such unbelievable, unconditional love. You were healthy, happy, and perfect."

I glance over again. Andy's smiling.

I go on. "But, understandably, my doctors were very concerned. Even though I had made it through your pregnancy, they said the next time would be worse. So your father and I made the very difficult decision to not have another child. And you became our world."

I hear Andy chuckle. I'm sure it's at the sappiness of the sentiment. I know he's not laughing at me.

We pull up to the driveway and wait for the gate to open.

"Y'know," Andy says, "Jos says her parents call her their 'heart.'"

I smile. "I like that."

"I should probably text her tonight, huh?" he says.

"That's up to you," I reply. "But I'm sure she would appreciate it."

We pull into the garage, and I turn off the car. I turn to Andy and place a hand on his cheek. "You will always be the most precious person in our lives," I say to him. "And I am truly very proud of the man you are becoming. Growing up isn't easy, regardless of what life throws your way. All we want—all we'll always want—is for you to be happy and to feel better."

Andy smiles. His cheeks flush slightly. "Thanks, Mom. I'll work on feeling better. I promise."

"I know you will," I say.

Andy

I go back to school on Wednesday, feeling a little bit better. I still have a few scratches on my face, but no one I talk to says anything. Apparently, someone reported to the principal that Julio and his buddies had attempted to attack me in the park, and they've been suspended for bullying, despite the fact that I probably hurt them more than they hurt me. I asked Dad yesterday when he got home if I needed to talk to the principal or anything, but he said everything was "copesetic," another of his ten-dollar words. Mom suggests I take a break from weights for a while until my headaches subside. I tell the guys at lunch I won't be joining them for a while. They understand and support my decision.

"I hate working out with headaches too," Mike says. I mean, he's not wrong.

I texted Joslyn last night and asked if she would be able to walk home with me after school. She sent me her classic reply.

OK :)

I wait for Joslyn in our usual spot outside the side entrance after school. I don't have any particular agenda. I figure we can just walk and see where our conversation takes us—how was your day, how did classes go, any new ideas, any gossip I should be aware of, etc. I'll save the talk about spring dance for another time.

I hear the doors open and Joslyn comes out, joined by her friends from her history class. She looks over at me, smiles, and waves. Man, I missed her smile. She then turns back to the door. Paul walks out, followed by Bruno. They all look up and see me, stopping just outside the door. Bruno turns to Paul and starts talking to him. He looks nervous. I guess I don't blame him, seeing as how I look like the bully now.

Joslyn comes up to me. I feel myself grow a stupid smile. Man, I *really* missed her.

"Bruno wants to talk to you if you feel up to it," she whispers to me.

I feel my smile fade.

Jos sees it, too, and quickly adds, "But if you're not we can just go now."

I look over at Bruno. He's super nervous. I look back to Joslyn and give her another smile. She smiles back.

I walk up to Bruno, Joslyn following close behind. I put out my hand. "Hey, man. Been a while."

Bruno shakes my hand cautiously. Then he smiles.

"How's it been?"

"Hey," he says. "Good to see you, man."

I look around at everyone. They're all smiling. Joslyn's wearing the best smile of everyone. The one I've missed for a while.

"I don't know which way y'all are walking," I say to everyone, "but you're welcome to come with us. We're just walking home." I look at Joslyn. "It's alright if we invite them, right?"

"Sure," she replies happily.

The group of us head off the school grounds. I quickly realize, this is the group of friends Jos has lunch with every day. I also realize, as I listen to everyone chatting, that Lauren is one of the bassists in the orchestra.

"You probably know my buddy, Sal," I say to her.

"Yeah," Lauren replies, a bit bashfully. "He's been helping to teach me how to play since I switched instruments. He's been super nice." Sal *really* needs to ask Lauren to the spring dance. I'll tell him tomorrow.

Paul and Lauren soon split off, and Riley follows shortly. Now it's just me, Joslyn, and Bruno. Joslyn is standing between us, and I catch her alternating glancing at us. Now *she's* super nervous.

"So," I say, turning to Bruno, "when'd you and your mom move back?"

"Last November," Bruno answers. "Mom had a really good job offer and took it."

"I heard rumors your dad basically skipped town," I say. I'd overheard Dad and Mom talking about it after we learned Bruno and his mom moved back. "That must be rough, man. I'm sorry to hear that."

"Eh, my dad's a piece of work," Bruno says dismissively. "I'm sorry it took me so long to realize that."

"Hey, you're not your dad," I reply. "I'm sorry it took *me* so long to realize that."

"That doesn't excuse everything I did to you in elementary school," Bruno says. "I don't think my mom knew how bad everything really was until that day where...y'know..."

"Yeah," I say, "I know."

"After we moved, she found a therapist for me," Bruno continues. "Turns out I had a lot going on. My dad wasn't punishing me for my actions, and it was messing me up. They said it was like some form of child abuse. I'm still working on getting it all sorted out, but with my dad out of the picture, it's been helpful."

"Yeah," I say. "I..." I look over at Joslyn. She looks away quickly. I think she's blushing. "I had a second antler incident a couple years ago. My parents found a therapist for me too. Talked with my mom yesterday about probably going back. Seems I still have some anger issues."

"Well," Bruno says, "at least you're still using your antlers to protect the people you care about." He looks over to Joslyn and smiles.

Joslyn is still looking at the sidewalk. And she's definitely blushing.

"I admired that about you," he adds, looking back up at me. "I remember that, when you got angry at my dad, it was because of what he had said about your folks and did to your dad. You were angry at him on their behalf. That was impressive."

Wow. I never thought I'd hear Bruno admit something like that to me. Someone who, all my life, I thought was a selfish pompous ass I never wanted to meet again. I feel so many feelings from just that statement, but none as sweet and wonderful as the feeling of Joslyn taking my hand. I look over at her again. She looks so happy and so proud.

I really, really missed her smile.

We get to Bruno's neighborhood and say our goodbyes. Now it's just me and Jos. And we're still holding hands.

We walk in silence, but we're both smiling stupidly. A few times, I feel her lean against my arm like she's nudging me playfully. I do the same to her, and she giggles. Now we're both blushing.

I walk her to her front door, but I don't want to let her hand go just yet. I look at her, her flushed cheeks, and her adorable smile.

"You're amazing," I say to her. "I don't know that I would have been able to talk to Bruno without you there."

"You're the one who walked up to him," she says to me. "You need to give yourself some credit."

"I've...been going through a lot these last few weeks," I say, taking her other hand. "Figuring out a lot about myself. I just want to thank you for always being there for me. I don't know that I always deserve it, but thank you." We just look at each other for another moment. Jos is so adorable when she's shy. "Would it be weird right now if I gave you a hug?" I ask. "I mean, I don't want to make you feel uncomfortable or anything."

"I would love a hug," she says.

I let go of her hands and put my arms around her. She puts hers around me, and I hold her tightly. I can't believe I have such a wonderful person, a wonderful friend like her in my life. She makes me so happy. I really don't want to let her go.

Just then her front door opens.

"Well now," her father says, and we quickly let go of each other and turn to face him. "What's going on here? You two sharing secrets or something?"

"Daddy!" Joslyn exclaims, embarrassed.

I just laugh and shake Mr. Harper's hand. "Good to see you, sir," I say. "Just walking Joslyn home is all."

"Well, feel free to come in if you'd like to share any more secrets or anything," Mr. Harper replies jokingly. "Just remember to keep your bedroom door open."

"Daddy!" Joslyn exclaims again.

"I actually should be heading home," I say.

"Alright. Good to see you. Tell your dad I said hi."

"Will do."

Mr. Harper goes back into the house, and Joslyn takes a step inside before turning back around.

"Yeah?" I ask.

"Let's go on a date this Friday," Joslyn says rather definitively. "Dinner and a movie after school. What do you think?"

"I think..." I start. "I think you stole my idea."

Joslyn giggles her cute giggle.

"Yes. Let's go on a date. After school on Friday."

"I can't wait," Joslyn says with great joy.

I really hope I never have to see that smile go away ever again.

* * *

We ask Dad if we can leave our things with him so we could just go on our date after school. Dad is so encouraging and so accommodating, I probably could've asked for his car keys, and he would have let us borrow it for the evening.

I don't, just in case he actually refused.

Our date starts with our usual Friday activity: getting coffee at our regular coffee shop and talking about our comic. Despite our emotional whirlwind journeys over the last week, we both still have ideas we hadn't shared about our story. Joslyn has the idea to flesh out the main character's backstory a bit more. It was probably our most creative and productive coffee in months.

"Can we start calling this our coffee date now too?" Jos asks.

"Sure," I reply. "Coffee Date Fridays. I like it!"

After our coffee date, we make our way to the mall. Dad let me use his rideshare account to take care of our transportation for us that evening (since I didn't ask to borrow his car). We first go to the movie theater to check out which movies are playing that evening. Joslyn points excitedly to one title in particular.

"They're playing the first *Sun Spot* movie as part of their sci-fi classics series tonight! Can we see it? Pleeeease? I've *always* wanted to see it in a theater."

"Isn't my mom in that?" I ask, even though I already know that she is. Jos nods enthusiastically. "Our second movie date, and you want to see another movie with my mom in it?"

"Pleeeease?" Jos pleads again.

I lean in and whisper, "She doesn't get naked in this one, does she?"

"Not this one, no," Joslyn answers. "In the second one, there's a little side-boob."

I shudder. "If we ever watch that one together, you're covering my eyes at that part," I say.

"Oh, I think they're playing it next week if you want to see," Joslyn says teasingly.

I just laugh and put my arm around her. Whatever makes her smile.

The movie doesn't start for a few hours, so we walk around the mall a bit, passing and pointing out stores we think we should apply to work at this summer. My parents said that I need to find a job if I want to pay to maintain my own car. Apparently, they've been negotiating with Gramma to give me her colorful station wagon so she can get a new hybrid. Mom says if I want anything nicer, like her Lexus or Dad's Volvo, I'll have to pay for it myself. Joslyn explains that her dad is working out the details to get her grandfather's old van so she can start using it to drive herself and friends around. "Daddy still really wants me to build a party van out of it," Jos says.

"You want help with that?" I offer. "I'll paint flying unicorns on the sides if you want."

Joslyn just giggles.

We get something to eat at one of the nicer food places in the mall before heading over to the theater to watch the movie. I knew Joslyn had seen *Sun Spot* several times, as it was truly one of her favorite movies. I've only seen it once maybe. This was the movie Mom shot just before *Grace Falls*.

We sit down in the theater and the movie comes on. I can't believe how young Mom looks. And her transformations are much more subtle. Definitely more toned down than in *Grace Falls*. I wondered if Mom ever considers going back into acting again. I should ask her.

After the movie, we get a ride back to my house. When we get inside, only the light in the kitchen is on. I take Joslyn to my favorite spot in the backyard where we put the new fire pit I got for Christmas. I plug in the string of lights Dad strung up for me. The lighting is so warm. Joslyn looks so pretty sitting on the bench in the golden light. The fire pit already has fresh logs stacked in it, and there's a note addressed to me sitting on top. I open it and read it out loud.

"Dear Andy and Joslyn," I read. "Hope you enjoyed your date night. We figured you'd want to light a fire after you came home. There's some drinks and snacks in the small fridge on the porch, so help yourself. Please put the fire out completely before you come inside. Love you both. Signed, Mom and Dad. P.S. If you're going to make out, please keep all articles of clothing on."

Joslyn laughs while I feel my whole body heat. I crumple up the note and use it as kindling to light the fire. Jos gets us a couple Pamplemousse La Croixs from the fridge. We sit close to each other on the bench and just watch the fire.

"Y'know," Joslyn says, "I don't think I realized how much of a real crush I had on you until about a few weeks ago."

"Same here," I admit. "I mean, if you can't tell, I'm stupid dense."

"That's alright," Joslyn says. "I was overthinking everything. Something Bruno said the other day. About you protecting the people you like. It's true, y'know."

"Yeah?"

"I don't know if I told you," she says, shifting in her seat, "but when we first moved to this area, I started at a different middle school. Somehow word got around that I wore makeup to hide my skin condition, and kids started making fun of me viciously. It brought back ugly memories from elementary school when the boys would make fun of my skin. It got so bad, my parents had to take me out of that middle school, and they enrolled me in your school. That first day we met, Mr. Castro noticed I was wearing makeup. He asked me if it was because of my skin. He said he noticed, because the color of my makeup was a little off from my actual skin color. Apparently, he used to do makeup in a past job. He actually helped me pick out a better foundation."

"Oh, I didn't know that," I say, "about Mr. Castro, I mean. He's such a great guy."

"I know," Joslyn says. "But anyway, that day in class, when you stopped all the kids from making comments when I had to wash my face, it felt like you saved my life. If all that teasing had happened again, I don't know what I would have done. I probably would have wanted to curl up and die."

"Oh, Jos." I put my drink down and put my arm around her.

I hold her close to my side, and she leans her head against my shoulder.

"You were my superhero that day," she continues. "And you just kept being a superhero. You brought me on awesome adventures, like seeing the premiere of *Grace Falls*, or like the time we went to that VIP event for that museum exhibit on the History of the Muse that your grandmother curated and presented. Like, that stuff was out of this world amazing! And you chose to include me. That made me just...so happy."

"You make me so happy too," I say to her. "You encourage me to be creative, you're honest with me when I need it, and you didn't judge me when you saw the worst of me. I...I still haven't gotten over that time I got angry and grew antlers in front of you. I thought I'd ruined our chance of being friends. I felt that way again when you saw me in the park. All I wanted to do was ask if you wanted to go to the spring dance with me."

"Yes," Joslyn says excitedly. "I do want to go with you to the dance!" I smile. She smiles. "But go on with your story."

"I guess my point is," I continue, "you stayed with me. You've seen the worst of me, and it hasn't scared you away. I don't know what you see in me all the time, but I want to see it. I want to be a better person for you. Because of you. I really do." I look Joslyn in the eyes. "Thank you for saving me."

I lean down a little. Joslyn raises her head a little. I smile. She smiles.

Then, finally, like I probably should've done a while ago, I kiss her.

And then she makes me the happiest boy in the whole world when she, in turn, kisses me back.

5

The Boy Who Grew Up

Rick

"How's your rewrites coming along?" I ask Abby as I sit down next to her in the living room.

"They're coming," she says, looking intently at her laptop. "I'm really trying to interpret and apply your feedback. Are you sure it's not too long-winded to completely detail my character's backstories?"

"It's always been a great exercise for me," I say, "even if it's just a reference for me. I can always take out what is too much. Have we heard from Andy yet? Do you know how late they'll be out?"

"He's over at Joslyn's, and they're picking everyone up," Abby answers. "The dance ends at ten, and I told him they could bring all their friends over to our place afterward, and they can all hang out in the backyard, as long as they don't drink alcohol or get naked or wake us up."

"Dammit, Mom," I retort, mimicking our son. "You're no fun."

"Just doing my job," she says with a knowing smile.

"By the way, have you thought of a title yet for your story?"

"I was thinking," she says, "'Morning Bloom.' What do you think? Too weird?"

Andy

Miss Monica insists on getting pictures of Jos and me before we leave for the dance. She says we're "too cute" together not to get some pictures before we get all hot and sweaty from dancing all night. Since when do high schoolers dance at dances?

We stand in Joslyn's sunroom next to her books and blooming angel wing begonias for nearly fifteen minutes, while her parents take approximately three thousand photos, occasionally sending one to a relative or even to my mom. As long as Joslyn's happy, I don't mind.

Gramma had gotten me a new collection of flat caps for Christmas. Ever since the night she brought Jos and me to see *Grace Falls*, when I had to wear one to hide my antler bald spots, she had been getting me a new one for every occasion she could think of. This time, though, she included matching bow ties and suspenders with each cap. I guess Gramma wants to pass down some of her style to me. Not that I mind, I love her style.

I had asked Jos if there was any hat/tie/suspender combination she preferred for the dance. She picked out a medium tan cap with a pattern of different colored crossing lines, like a check or plaid pattern; a matching pair of tan suspenders with threads of red, blue, yellow, and green; and a burgundy bowtie that matched the flowers in her dress. I have truly never felt so formal or disgustingly hipster. I actually kinda like it.

The real flower, though, is Joslyn herself. She looks stunning in her petticoat dress, and her makeup is flawless. She knows I don't care if she wears her foundation or not, but when she does up her eyes, blush, and lips, she's breathtaking. I can't believe I have such a beautiful girl in my life, and on my arm, tonight. And I can't believe how excited I am thinking of bringing her to prom next year. I never thought I'd actually be looking forward to school dances.

Once we're finally released from the photoshoot, we get into Joslyn's "new" van and take off to pick up all our friends and head to the dance. We start by picking up Bruno and Tracy, then Paul, Jason, Maxine, Mike, Riley, then Lauren and Sal. I'm sure we've overpacked the van, but everyone seems fine crammed into all the seats. I sit in the passenger seat, as Joslyn safely drives our cohort to our school for the dance. We joke about ways we can turn Jos's van into a real party van and everything we'd have to add, remove, or remodel to do so. Basically, it boils down to better speakers and more lights.

We arrive at school and make our way to the auditorium. As expected, the "dance" is mostly just groups of people huddling together, but dressed a little nicer than usual. Jos and I stick together the entire time as members of our group break off to dance or hang with other groups. We comment on how Tracy and Bruno look like they've really hit it off. Bruno is acting like such a gentleman to her, getting her drinks and tagging along with her when she wants to talk to other people. And she looks proud to have him with her too. Almost like she's showing him off.

I'm really proud to see Lauren and Sal enjoying each other's company too. It took a week of persuasion to finally get Sal to ask Lauren if she wanted to go to the dance with him. It took Lauren less than twenty-four hours to accept his request.

Mike's chatting up Maxine and Riley most of the night, showing off his muscles and generally trying to make them laugh. They actually seem to enjoy his antics.

I don't know how, but Paul and Jason somehow manage to pull Bruno and me onto the dance floor with a bunch of other guys, to do one of those Korean dance fads that's apparently been popular recently. Joslyn and the other girls cheer us on as we "perform." I don't know what I'm doing, but it makes Jos happy, and that's all I really want to do.

Then the last slow dance of the night plays, and Joslyn pulls me onto the dance floor. She doesn't have to pull very hard. She puts her arms over my shoulders, and I gently hold her waist. We just start stepping side to side with the music while we look at each other, smiling.

"Thank you so much for coming with me," she says. "This was a lot more fun than I thought."

"I'm really glad I came with you," I say. "I would have missed out if I didn't. Thank you for asking me."

"Have you thought at all what you want to do after high school?" she asks. An odd conversation to start at a school dance, but sure.

"Not entirely," I say. "Dad definitely wants me to start thinking about careers and colleges, and if that's what I want to do. Have you thought about it?"

"A little," she says. "I definitely want to continue doing

something creative. Was thinking of talking to your dad about screenwriting and where I could go to learn more about that."

"That sounds perfect for you," I say. "And I bet he'd be happy to help."

"Do you think you'd want to move away or anything after high school?" she asks.

"Really haven't thought about it," I say honestly. "I'm actually finally enjoying high school and having friends. Figured I'd enjoy this for now, especially since you're here."

Joslyn smiles super wide. So do I.

I pull Joslyn in a little closer as the song starts to come to an end. She places her head on my chest, and I put my chin on her head. We just continue to step and sway side to side. I look around the dance floor: Bruno's dancing and chatting with Tracy, Sal and Lauren are exchanging goofy smiles while they dance, and Mike's still chatting up Riley and Maxine near the punch bowl. Everyone's doing alright.

Then I look back down at the beautiful head of hair, like soft springs, I have on my chest. I don't know that I've ever been happier.

After the slow dance, we gather everyone in our cohort and head back to my house to hang out for the rest of the night. We pull up the driveway, and I let everyone in. Mom and Dad are still in the living room. Dad's reading through assignments, and Mom's working on her writing. I introduce everyone to my parents and let the few who haven't yet met my famous mother gush over her for a bit. I get the feeling Mom's actually enjoying all of it.

Mom's especially happy to see Bruno again. She gives him a long warm hug and comments on how handsome he's become.

"A hundred times more handsome than your dad," she says. And she means it.

Bruno smiles and blushes. "Thanks, Miss Andrews," he says bashfully.

The guys help me move my firepit out a bit so we can set up more chairs, while Jos and the others get snacks and drinks for everyone. We all sit around the fire and talk and chat about everything. We talk about the dance, about our favorite movies, our favorite music, our favorite memories from elementary and middle school. We debate our favorite TV shows and comic book heroes, we compare our favorite books and video games, we share new ideas and recommendations on what places to visit and what to eat. We have a great time.

It took me my whole childhood, but I think I've finally found it. I've found my happiness, especially my happiness with others. I've found my outlet. I've found my friends.

And I found Joslyn. The girl who grew wings and saved the world. Or rather, the girl who found me and liked me for who I am. I look at her. She's talking and laughing with Tracy and Riley. She looks so happy and so beautiful. She looks up at me and smiles. Oh, Joslyn, I hope that smile never disappears from my life ever again.

We hear rustling in the woods behind the house. Paul turns on the flashlight on his phone and points it toward the sound.

"What is that?" Mike asks.

"Oh!" I say. "That's a white-tailed buck. There are a few that live in the woods back there. They'll sometimes come out to eat the brush. That one's probably about five or six years old."

"How can you tell?" Mike asks.

"Easy," I say, "you can tell by the antlers."